The *Best*
AUSTRALIAN POETRY
2006

THE BEST AUSTRALIAN POETRY SERIES

The Best Australian Poetry 2005
Guest Editor: Peter Porter

The Best Australian Poetry 2004
Guest Editor: Anthony Lawrence

The Best Australian Poetry 2003
Guest Editor: Martin Duwell

The Best AUSTRALIAN POETRY 2006

Guest Editor
JUDITH BEVERIDGE

SERIES EDITORS

BRONWYN LEA & MARTIN DUWELL

UQP

First published 2006 by University of Queensland Press
PO Box 6042, St Lucia, Queensland 4067 Australia

www.uqp.uq.edu.au

Typeset in 11/16pt Times by Post Pre-Press Group, Brisbane
Printed in Australia by McPherson's Printing Group

This project has been assisted by
the Commonwealth Government through
the Australia Council, its arts funding
and advisory body.

This publication is proudly sponsored by the Josephine Ulrick and
Win Schubert Foundation for the Arts.

Cover painting by Michael Zavros, *Spring/Fall 11* (detail), 2004, Oil on Canvas
(210 x 167 cm), courtesy of the artist and Schubert Contemporary

Cataloguing in Publication Data
National Library of Australia

The best Australian poetry 2006.

   1. Australian poetry – 21st century – Collections
   I. Duwell, Martin, 1948–. II. Lea, Bronwyn, 1969–.

A821.4

ISBN 0 7022 3568 7

Contents

Bronwyn Lea and Martin Duwell

Foreword

It should cause no surprise that Judith Beveridge, the editor of the fourth collection in our *Best Australian Poetry* series, has produced such a satisfying and stimulating selection. Those two adjectives accurately summarise the effect of her own work which has grown steadily in public esteem to the point where she can now be seen as one of Australia's leading poets. Beveridge's three books of poems have, between them, received many of Australia's major poetry awards – including the New South Wales Premier's Award, the Victorian Premier's Award and the Judith Wright Calanthe Poetry Prize – and each book has managed to pull off that complicated coup of being pleasing to both the literary critic and lay reader alike. Her most recent collection, *Wolf Notes*, brings together a number of her poetic preoccupations – music, portraiture, affiliations between the human and nonhuman worlds, Buddhism – and contains the prize-winning sequence 'Between the Palace and the Bodhi Tree', which explores how one consciousness awoke and shows how the 2,500-year-old teachings of Siddhartha are still pertinent today. A reader acquainted with Beveridge's poems will find them immediately recognisable by the way she pressures and plays with language, giving the sense that each word has been necessarily carved out of silence and selected with care.

In making her selection for this year's anthology, Beveridge has searched, as she tells us in her introduction, for poems in which the poets have won a battle with language rather than simply exploited comfortable idioms or, as she puts it, have 'sat back on their comfortable haunches and written from facility or clannish pride'. As a result this anthology has a high percentage of poems which at first reading might be puzzling to some but which are attractive enough to lure the reader into the kind of deeper engagement that rewards us with rich responses. And as a result of this there is a high percentage of memorable poems here. Sometimes our initial puzzlement derives from an uncertainty as to what the poem is doing, how it is approaching its subject. The first and last poems of the book are examples of this. Robert Adamson's 'A Visitation', describes with deceptive simplicity how, after a forty-year hiatus, the poet once again sees a yellow-footed rock wallaby: this time, one which has survived a Sydney bush fire. And we are not sure whether we are reading about an image that represents those humans who have been damaged by the intensity of exposure to the gods – what Patrick White, borrowing from Greek culture, called 'The Burnt Ones' – or whether we are seeing what is, for the poet, a bearer of revelation, a reminder to someone who has left childhood far behind, of the overwhelming wildness of the natural world. And '*I giorni della merla*' (the days of the blackbird) by Simon West – the poem with which Beveridge's selection concludes – is also about visitations. Here January's blackbirds promise some kind of revelation but withhold themselves. Those who with tired stares 'await the wasn't of a century' – a beautiful phrase – know the bird only as a shape in their minds.

This is also an anthology of mysterious narratives; a genre that emerges every so often in Beveridge's own work. They can be surreal/symbolic stories like Peter Rose's 'Beach Burial', Alex Skovron's 'Sorcery', Kathleen Stewart's 'How I Got Away' or Barbara Temperton's 'The Lighthouse Keeper's

Wife' (a very Beveridgean poem). Equally they can be fairly straightforward narrations of what would be, to most of us, a surreal reality: Philip Salom's '*sections from* The Man with a Shattered World' describes the psychic fate of an actual Russian soldier who lost the left side of his brain and Lesley Walter's 'Hyphenated Lives' tells the true and remarkable story of a pair of Siamese twins who produced a total of twenty-one children. All in all, Beveridge has done what we want our guest editors to do: to produce a selection which reflects the editor's tastes and obsessions (this book is full of moons and horses) and yet have a coherent position on the question of what good poems in Australia should do. The result is one of the liveliest gatherings of Australian poetry we have read.

On a less happy note, last year was marked by extensive depredations by the Angel of Death among Australian poets. Tasmanian writers Barney Roberts, Jenny Boult and Margaret Scott all passed away. Margaret Scott's work has been celebrated recently in an excellent article by Ruth Blair, 'Finding Home: The Poetry of Margaret Scott' (*Australian Literary Studies* 22.2), which shows how Scott's migrant experience (she moved to Australia from England in 1959) forms a subtle framework that can be seen to encompass all her thematic material: in particular, the idea of home, which in all its guises is a recurrent focus in her poems. Scott published five books of poetry including a *Collected Poems* in 2000 (Montpelier).

Two Melbournian poets, Philip Martin and Shelton Lea, also passed away. The former after a long and debilitating illness; the latter after a long and lively life. Philip Martin's *Voice Unaccompanied*, though a late first book, has many virtues and is one of those books which looks better as time goes on. Shelton Lea is still remembered in Queensland for a tempestuous visit in 1974. It produced a book in the Makar Press, Gargoyle Poets series called *Chockablock with Dawn* and one of us still has one of Lea's chapbooks in which the author inscribed 'Thanks for the American Dollar, Kid'. This referred to some overseas currency which had been lying around in the Makar Press Office and which was exchanged for a book which we hadn't the courage to refuse. But Michael Sharkey in an obituary in *Overland* speaks of their long relationship and writes so eloquently that it is impossible not to believe his account of Shelton Lea as someone:

> [who] had the least sense of imposition, the surest sense that people would see a charitable act required doing and would do it. I think he had the least malicious intentions of anyone I've met. His self-deprecation was boundless, his awareness that he was putting on an act so surely judged ('How was I, brudder?'; 'Could you believe that?') that it was impossible to begrudge him anything.

A final victim was the Canberra poet Michael Thwaites who, between the ages of thirty-five and fifty-six, worked for Australia's security intelligence organisation (ASIO). He went on to publish five collections of poetry but is best known for the story in which ASIO's director-general Charles Spry recruited him saying, 'You write poetry, I know. Much of the job will just be hard methodical work but imagination is also needed. I believe you could make a valuable contribution', thereby establishing the possibility of a new kind of social relevance for poetry in Australia.

GUEST EDITOR

JUDITH BEVERIDGE

Judith Beveridge was born in London in 1956 and migrated to Australia in 1960 on the assisted passage scheme. On arriving in Australia, her family settled for a time in Carlingford, then a rural suburb of Sydney and also where her grandparents lived. The family then moved to North Auburn, a working-class, industrial suburb situated in Sydney's west. She attended primary and high schools in Auburn and Parramatta respectively. Suffering from severe shyness as a child she often retreated into the world of the imagination and books, and her interest in poetry developed from an early age, her earliest influences being Robert Louis Stevenson and D H Lawrence. She remembers, at the age of twelve, constantly carrying a copy of the *Iliad* around with her simply because she loved the name of the book and the idea that it may have been written by a blind bard.

After finishing high school she studied at the University of Technology, Sydney, one of the first institutions at that time to have a writing degree. There she was encouraged in her writing by Arnie Goldman and was one of the editors of the literary journal *Free Seeds*. After finishing her degree she worked part-time in offices and libraries while she wrote her first book of poems, *The Domesticity of Giraffes*, which was published by Black Lightning Press in 1987. In 1988 it received the Dame Mary Gilmore Award, the NSW Premier's Poetry Prize and the Victorian Premier's Poetry Prize. Poems from that volume were subsequently put on the HSC curriculum. In 1995 she edited with Jill Jones and Louise Wakeling, *A Parachute of*

Blue, an anthology of Australian poetry. She has also worked on the literary magazines *Hobo* and *Kalimat* and is the current poetry editor of *Meanjin*. In 1989 her son Phillip was born and she did not resume her poetry writing until 1992. She published her second volume, *Accidental Grace*, with UQP in 1996, and it won the Wesley Michel Wright Award and was shortlisted for other awards. During 1991 and 1996 she travelled in India, England and Germany with her husband and son. On her return, she worked at a number of part-time jobs including bush regeneration, teaching and library work. In 1999 she attended the International Poetry Festival in Medellin in Colombia, and in 2003 was one of ten poets invited to Berlin to participate in the poetry translation project. In 2003 she published her third volume of poetry, *Wolf Notes*, with Giramondo Publishing. In 2004 it won the Judith Wright Calanthe Award for Poetry and the Victorian Premier's Poetry Prize. In 2005 she was awarded the Philip Hodgins Memorial Medal for excellence in literature. Since 2002 she has been teaching poetry-writing at postgraduate level at Sydney University, having also worked for a time at Newcastle University. She has written reviews and articles for major literary journals. From 2001–2004 she was a member of the Literature Board of the Australia Council. Her poetry has been translated into several languages including Arabic, Chinese, German and Spanish. She continues to live in Sydney with her partner Stephen Edgar.

JUDITH BEVERIDGE

INTRODUCTION

Like many Australians, each dawn I am woken by the flocks of sulphur-crested cockatoos as they leave their hollows and branches to begin their day. Some mornings the noise can be horrendous – I've only just recently moved to this heavily treed suburb of Sydney, and I suppose I'll eventually learn to sleep through the birds' early morning mafficking – but for now, these metal-throated birds excavate my sleep. But there is something funny. Within that rattlebox flock there is one cockatoo whose call is distinct and separate from the others. And when I hear it I am amused, amazed, bewildered, and, in a strange way, reminded of the poet – that maverick voice breaking step with the rest. The sound this cockatoo makes suggests that its story is sorrier, more besetting than that of its flock-mates: for it must once have been someone's pet, and thus confined to a cage. Whoever kept it has taught it to say 'ribbit ribbit' – as though it were a cartoon frog. And so, many times each day I hear its loud 'ribbit ribbit' as it passes across the sky, or settles down for a while in one of the gum trees' high branches. I often wonder what the other cockatoos make of it, and I also marvel at the fact that it hasn't discarded this call, despite its now being part of a flock and free to be raucous.

When the pile of poems from UQP arrived on my doorstep, I felt a wave of irritation pass over me as if I'd just been woken up by another loud flock. So many voices – how will I sift through, how will I choose? I knew that out of this large bundle a number of anthologies could be selected – that there would be enough good material and enough variety to make more than just one anthology. The difficulty would be in deciding what *particular* type of anthology to select. I had to ask myself what it was that I most wanted to say about the nature of poetry through my selection; with what was I going to beckon the reader? I thought of that cockatoo and of what it said about the keeper who had taught it the comic 'ribbit ribbit'. If you are going to go to the trouble to teach a bird to speak, you're going to teach it something poignant, humorous, or colourful, depending on your own proclivities and mettle.

Choosing the poems forced me to think hard about what it was I wanted the anthology to say about the nature of poetry, given that numerous anthologies and thus numerous ideas about poetry could be constructed out of the pile. I could certainly have made a number of anthologies that made poetry wear the motley well, as poetry, like music, is broad in reach and manner, and I was particularly impressed, after reading through the poems, by the variety of poems being written today. There is nothing worse than a homogeneity of styles, and though Australian poets share a community of descent, it speaks well that so many poets are finding new and interesting ways of using influence, innovation, tradition, form, voice – but I knew that flourish and mode were not what I wanted to showcase, as there can also be nothing worse than an anthology that is simply a loose hotchpotch – all ingredients and no meal.

I decided that my main criteria of selection would be for poems which showed that the poet had an engaged, vital, deep relationship with language; no easy, or given one – but a relationship that over time has been hard won. I'm sure too that this is one of the reasons why my selection tends to favour established writers over the new. If a poet has not tried to work out their precise relationship with language, then they will simply not be able to deliver latency, compression, authenticity, power – obviously this takes time and experience – yet some of my own favourite poems in the anthology have been written by new/young poets. I looked for poems in which there was clear evidence that the poet had not just sat back on their comfortable haunches and written from facility or clannish pride. I wanted poems that showed a thorough coming to terms with the difficulty of circumscribing a position within the dark maw of words.

A poet needs a strange and compelling voice. More often than not, the relationship of the poet to language is like that of a surly step-child forever trying to find comfortable placement or kinship, but who is defined more by counter-position, contrariety and conflict when they meet the agency of words. I wanted poems that suggested a whole different (even difficult) history with language: poems that speak out much like the 'rib-bit bird' from the flock, even though that bird will be forever unaware of the meaning its keeper has imposed on it, making it a character in a human drama by particularising it.

Language can be a cruel keeper of dramatic ironies within the poet's life and part of the struggle the poet has is in foiling this. I believe poetry must always be a serious showdown between the word and the poet. All the poems in this anthology I believe have the gist and pith, the sum and substance of work that has endured a costly process. There are many ways to have a relationship with language – through form, rhythm, deportment of sentence, structure, line, image, diction. I believe the poems I have chosen for this anthology are outstanding for the ways in which they have come to terms with problems inherent in their subjects, poems which enter and commit to the transfiguring power of the imagination and whose impulses seem not to be supplanted by casualness or complacency born easily out of facilities and gifts. In one way or another, every one of these poets writes their poem as urgently and imperatively as if a death clause had been forged into the contract with their poem – do it well, poet, or fall on your sword.

Pablo Neruda in his *Memoirs* says this: *I love words so much . . . The unexpected ones . . . the ones I wait for greedily or stalk until, suddenly, they drop . . . Vowels I love . . . They glitter like coloured stones, they leap like silver fish, they are foam, thread, metal, dew . . . I run after certain words . . . They are so beautiful that I want to fit them all into my poem . . . I catch them in mid-flight, as they buzz past, I trap them, clean them, peel them, I set myself in front of the dish, they have a crystalline texture to me, vibrant, ivory, vegetable, oily, like fruit, like algae, like agates, like olives . . . And then I stir them, shake them, I drink them, I gulp them down, I mash them, I garnish them, I let them go . . . I leave them in my poem like stalactites, like slivers of polished wood, like coals, pickings from a shipwreck, gifts from the waves . . . Everything exists in the word.*[1]

I decided I would choose poems which simply made me do a double take, which held my attention by an ardent, deep-longing connection with the possibilities of language. In short, poems which were returning to language as a kind of enchantment and magic. This is not to suggest that I looked for poems which used complex, sophisticated or arcane methods and vocabularies, as some of the best poems are made up of very simple words; I simply wanted the poems which were using ordinary words in ways that were rich and strange.

Of the forty poems I have chosen there is a wide variety of themes, though curiously, when I read through the final selection, I noticed that seven out of the forty poems cite or develop

---

[1]Pablo Neruda, *Memoirs*. Trans. Hardie St. Martin. (New York: Farrar Straus and Giroux, 1977): 53.

scenarios with horses. This is either just one of those antics of chance, or the selection process also picking out certain of my own subliminal motifs as I was winnowing the pile. I was certainly very cognisant of the fact that I was reading for an anthology, and not just for a collection of individual poems, and therefore sweep and grandeur, yet also accord and unity would be virtues towards it. I am aware, too, that my watermark stains or impresses every page; that this particular selection is a stamp of my own sensibility and thoughts about certain approaches to writing; that I am a keeper wielding a particular line.

However, I am dazzled by a very great number of these poems. Judith Bishop's 'Rabbit' took my breath away for the way she can magically manoeuvre her sentences across lines and write with such poise and beauty. Stephen Edgar, Alan Gould and David Musgrave show how, in skilful hands, emotion can be dynamically yoked to form, how one of poetry's most enduring pleasures is how it can give to experience investigative shapes. The poems by Kevin Gillam and Jane Gibian, struck me for their lyrical and associative power, while Danny Gentile's poem 'The Lenten Veil' shares something with both Dickinson and Stevens for the way he makes his language and form appeal to the senses and yet also bear the mental tension of a volatile imagination. I was also struck by the reflective, resourceful way Martin Harrison drew me in to his poem, 'About the Self', through the conversational form and rhythms as they enacted, queried, amplified and enhanced. Gig Ryan, Peter Minter, Peter Porter, as sure-footed as ever in their poems, fuse culture, history, landscape into spellbinding textures and exhibit a mastery of language which I hope will attract and compel readers enough to bear with the demands their poems make. Meredith Wattison's, Jason Nelson's and Philip Hammial's poems enact with great flair William Carlos

Williams' injunction: 'If it ain't a pleasure, it ain't a poem.' Philip Harvey's amazing 'Non-core Promise' delivers humour and poignant political comment in his impressive ability to pun, mutate and wrangle layers of meaning out of the sound implications of words. That simplicity, clarity and directness can be virtues in poetry comes through in Dorothy Porter's potent, intense 'Waterview Street', and in Kevin Hart's luminous and wise 'The Word' which tells us how difficult it is to shape anything outside proprieties of what is easy and common.

All the poets in this anthology have made the difficult push into themselves to find the place and space where words can no longer lie shrivelled from the daily handling by many social, political and mercantile discourses. As Kevin Hart says: 'Your mouth is dark. Go far into yourself/ Let quietness gather there, then say the word.' I feel that these forty poems 'say the word'; that they give us back language uncontaminated, a space where feeling, perception, thought, imagination, word can all dovetail and become a threshold for connection and interconnection, rather than for division and separation. There's a terrific kind of exhilaration when you read a good poem, you know that the energy it brings comes from the questioning that has been launched somewhere in another's heart and mind about the human spirit, but there comes with it too a sense of loss. It's like the feeling I get whenever I hear the 'ribbit bird' (and I've heard it a few thousand times by now) – each time I am thrilled, disturbed, amazed – happy, and yet also sad because I think of what it cost the bird to be so separate in its call. A good, distinctive voice has its price and I would like to thank the poets for undergoing whatever it took for them to write these distinctive poems.

ROBERT ADAMSON

A VISITATION

All night wild fire burned in the tree-tops
on the other side of the river – now
it's morning and smoking embers
from the angophoras are landing in a clearing
on the near shore. A yellow-footed rock
wallaby limps in from the bush,
dazed with mucked fur, its tail hardly able
to support its weight. Although
wounded, it seems miraculous
as the morning sun catches the yellow hue
of its feet above black claws.
It's the first yellow-footer I've seen for more
than 40 years – and reminds me
of a time as a kid when I rowed
my grandfather's tallow-wood skiff across
Big Bay. There was a mob of four
rock wallabies, standing there as the boat
was pulled silently by the tide along
the shore. One I noticed, by the mottled fur
on its back, seemed to have mange,
like the river foxes of those days.
A panic suddenly ran through them
and the largest buck almost flew
straight up an enormous rock. It was sheer wildness,

so fierce it shocked me. Afterwards
the atmosphere was thick and I could smell
an odour unlike anything I recognised.
This morning, once again, that scent was in the air.
I turned to look but the wallaby had gone.

The Weekend Australian

LUKE BEESLEY

THE FIGHT

To talk plainly, now, about the day or the people crossing it.

The weather too; the warmth of a new season pressing on the early morning: too much heat in the bed and kicking to a cooler spot within sleep. The careful knowing of the heart. Of things. A mouth around a cup, the temperature of water or the temperature of the room – to think these things out: rooms, heat, something he or she said, the idea of *room* temperature . . .

There are fighters. The belts around their waists are blue.

They will have a mock fight – a spar. It is a large kitchen and the morning is gathering pace, placing itself down on the hill and the mountain gently and eventually to the really slow place of the house on the edge of the cliff, in truth, and gradually filling with people: the town, the tourist, a priest.

We listen from the lounge to the swift thick flap of their garments, the rush of air from their lungs. The kitchen. We have to imagine. The hit. They practise while the town leans close. It is winter and you wait on the thick green lawn. Look at the tiger. Lilies. The garden shifting gently, clemency; the temperature of an arm the hot spine the swift shape of alphabet spelling: *you've fallen,* and later, *can you hear me?*

One at a time we know it is finished.

Your sister calls (to come) and you know, and the flower you keep in your hand. And the long trial (a goose for each person), a cloud as a biscuit or a person on the last train home. It is August and the waiter says *karate* instead of *latté* and you kick him underneath the table. You need it.

Heat

Judith Bishop

RABBIT

Life shivers between yourself and us: help us to stretch
toward the kingdom of our burrows in the earth: we'll never
    occupy
again the silk-soft that was a womb, but we wander the night
    grass with you,
searching for a tenderness, an innocence at birth: until the
    quiet winds cut
the quiet breath from your mouth and your hindquarters
    stamp, *Quickly, I must go –*

Rabbit, winding up your stride, in your alignment, recalling
    full stretch,
a god's arrow-head, shaft, lengthening from nose to tail,
    aching to occupy
the whole damn bubble of the moment of each movement: if you
made it, what would snap, whose shining fingers, what scene
    would cut
abruptly to another, what deity float gently in to bid us her
    good night?

Rabbit, laid ragged at the fold of day's field, where the
    sparrow-hawk stretched
the stars' scarf across her wing: with your velvet heart, you
    occupied
the blood's old theatre: with your hushed ballet of spring, you
performed the coiled rites you have taught us tonight: showed
    our ropes of matter cut
by the one puppet-master, hanging in his own winds.

Australian Book Review

STEPHEN EDGAR

MAN ON THE MOON

Hardly a feature in the evening sky
As yet – near the horizon the cold glow
Of rose and mauve which, as you look on high,
Deepens to Giotto's dream of indigo.

Hardly a star as yet. And then that frail
Sliver of moon like a thin peel of soap
Gouged by a nail, or the paring of a nail:
Slender enough repository of hope.

There was no lack of hope when thirty-five
Full years ago they sent up the *Apollo* –
Two thirds of all the years I've been alive.
They let us out of school, so we could follow

The broadcast of that memorable scene,
Crouching in Mr Langshaw's tiny flat,
The whole class huddled round the TV screen.
There's not much chance, then, of forgetting that.

And for the first time ever I think now,
As though it were a memory, that you
Were in the world then and alive, and how
Down time's long labyrinthine avenue

Eventually you'd bring yourself to me,
With no excessive haste and none too soon –
As memorable in my history
As that small step for man onto the moon.

How pitiful and inveterate the way
We view the paths by which our lives descended
From the far past down to the present day
And fancy those contingencies intended,

A secret destiny planned in advance
Where what is done is as it must be done
For us alone. When really it's all chance
And the special one might have been anyone.

The paths that I imagined to have come
Together and for good have simply crossed
And carried on. And that delirium
We found is cold and sober now and lost.

The crescent moon, to quote myself, lies back,
A radiotelescope propped to receive
The signals of the circling zodiac.
I send my thoughts up, wishing to believe

That they might strike the moon and be transferred
To where you are and find or join your own.
Don't smile. I know the notion is absurd,
And everything I think, I think alone.

Australian Book Review

Danny Gentile

THE LENTEN VEIL

A shift of the peripheral distracts the weather
eye. It distracts with its uncertain lines. It has
a loose mobility like a feather falling from a
tree. As such it is a shift into asymmetry. There,

a confabulation can occur & be identified. Wash
off the exterior in a basinful of water & let your
face collect the air. Sit by the open window &
watch the clouds recover. The breeze feels clean

though salty. It does not waver from you in
your penitent frame. It does not lift the corners
of tea-towels on the clothesline. The breath is
not strong – the feather & leaf do not define

the tree. It is not your way to give succour to
the callings of Ash Wednesday, as palm fronds
have been burnt to give a thumbprint – a stain.
The face of the priest comes back to your grey –

grey. But you long since offered him sympathy
in the leadlight refectory where he kneels –
sighs – abdicates. The arrangement of his bones
reverberates the crepitus of age. In his sighing

sits a yearning for the spirit to decay. Let it
give way like some shrugging thing. Weights
have been lifted & the air become dry of God.
It seems feather & shadow alone have shifted.

Meanjin

JANE GIBIAN

ARDENT

Something glides on the smile of the knife
Like a swan dreamily skimming the surface of the lake
— NGUYỄN QUANG THIỀU

You wanted everything, to hold it all: the precise
measure of tears filling each eye, to ingest
parts of a concerto into the body: you want
a locked box for the scraps of paper, that recipe

of ideas; a treasure chest to quarantine your heart –
but already it's the time of dahlias, the ending
of the time of sunflowers; almost the reign
of goannas, when the birds call unmistakeable

warnings to one another. You needed to zoom in
so closely a sprig of lavender became myriad
tiny blooms bursting in spirals; you had to lick
the knife blade. Waking cut like a sword,

clambering from the dream of a soldier leaving –
she was pressing her cheek against the cotton chest
of a tall man, faceless, inhaling serenity and amaranth;
the lull, the surrender into a dark smudge of sleep.

The ardent harbour exploding with infinite stars:
you tried to hold it all – like the knife between
your teeth, it's a trapdoor into the night now:
under the clipped fingernail of a moon, you find
yourself staring straight into the eyes of an owl.

_____

Heat

KEVIN GILLAM

'LOW AT THE EDGE OF THE SANDS'

they told me I wouldn't find you
yet I find you everywhere.
when you spoke; value of flotsam,
the quick note, calicoed thievery.
now this, weedy seadragon, lifted
from a mizzled island,
body of curves, a question mark.
and I'm in memory's spume,
your stooped body no less questioning,
no less colourful, sinewy, then brittling.
perhaps (not a word you employed much,
always more percussive than perhaps)
you were to page as this was to reef.
a traveller, strong sense of home,
untroubled at not being understood.
they told me of white ants,
slow truth of bone.
in this fraught wind-whipped
weather, the distinction between
sea and sky not clear
I am stilled talking to water

for you spoke in a clutter of tongues,
religion of purpose,

never rain but spiderings of drizzle,
sudden applause on tin,
drenchings of man and map.
this dragon too, a salt-infused fiction
of instinct and need,
unfurled for a last time,
plot laid bare.
in thin dreams of meadowgrass
you both feeding, being.
I am humbled, in soft focus,
sifting word and kelp from brine
though language, like your
rainbowed skin bleeding
through my fingers
seeks the familiarity of now.
was it time
or the diseased sea?
I am still talking to water.
they said it would be so

Australian Book Review

ALAN GOULD

IRIS

I will not give this day to God, or to God's ilk,
though day falls open, blue and yolk
like an iris. Not to God, neither to Null,
though the air is cool
first-morning of the world above
Mount Majura's script of trees and fences
which are expressions, sure, of different loves.

If the fence is where agnostics sit,
better there than in the lea of it,
I tell the man who wades into the stream,
wanting to rescue my unbelief from dream.

Birth, kids and death,
I'll wear my refusal to live within a faith,
wear *and* work it, and maybe test its worth,
or die pedestrian.

But will concede this. The quarrel, 'What
is existence for?' is a fight I have
with God or the God-mirror, is no business of
any person with like mind to me or not.

I will not give the day to God, nor otherwise,
whatever iris-miracle arrests my eyes.
Yet cusp, crisp and electric tilts this sunrise
toward what?
                    Some self-arousal I approve?
For sure, creation finds in me some buoyant love,
no more, maybe, than what the creatures have,
as I take in the tele-warble of the birdsong
that carols, quarrels, but will not harangue.

Blue Dog: Australian Poetry

PHILIP HAMMIAL

WATER

Die as much as you want. An inch
at a time or all at once, it doesn't matter. Your conviction
that the new Human Tissue Bill will somehow protect you
is a delusion. Take it from me, I know. It's
not for nothing that I've been an envoy to the Mahdi
for the past two years. Here to save us
from ourselves, his army's contribution
to our once-beautiful city is, according
to a recent poll, extremely disappointing, that
contribution having been, to date, one point two
million black parasols, one
for every male citizen. If only
it would rain. What a sight for sore eyes
it would be to watch those parasols blossoming
up & down the length of the Avenue Foch. Fat
chance. The drought
is here to stay. It's only a matter of time
before we pack our bags & head inland
to the great fresh water sea that supposedly covers
the heart of our continent. A rumour? Do you
know anyone who has actually seen it? I don't. Harry Kline
in his seminal work, *Paradise Now*, describes that sea
in detail – abundant with fish, barges poled by djinns
who are delighted to attend to your every need, etc. But

is Harry to be believed? What if he's sold out, become
another of the Mahdi's innumerable stooges? Considering
how quickly his book rose (was pushed) to the top
of the best-seller list, I'd say he probably is. All
things considered, if I were you
I'd do it all at once.

_____

Famous Reporter

JENNIFER HARRISON

THE TASTE OF HOURS

Tonight the husk of depression
rebels against the dark's philanthropy.
Nothing floats away.
This action might be enough,
that one too difficult –
but the high horse has no stirrups
the flank, slippery.
See how I walk down the hall
and disappear? How I sleep
in a room of lost garments?
Before the fist in my breast relaxes
what do the lungs demand?
What catches in the trees
when a storm sways through the branches?
Nothing floats away.
Mothers notice their children
invisible a moment before.
I won't be seduced by the taste of hours
but by you, weighing my body down
tenderness piercing bone
where trust lets the nerve through.

Blast Magazine

MARTIN HARRISON

ABOUT THE SELF

I'm somewhere near the Norfolk coast
in the back of a car.
I'm twenty-one. I'm still hung over
from last night's drugs. (In fact, wine mostly.) That's why I'm
    fixed
on the glinting sun-spandrels bursting the tunnel of
    overarching English trees,
then mirroring themselves in the slanting rear window –
I'm thinking how topsy-turvy the world is, how sky is anywhere,
how blueness jags into the earth. A difficult connection
with the girl in the front passenger seat is what I know as love:
we've just spent the night together, immersed in each other,
longing for each other's body, tumbling against each other,
jostling the night-spasms and judderings
of entry and thrust and pleasuring occurring minute by minute,
each burst making our carpet of stars. All night,
our night was touched with dark. That darkness, too,
was pale with flesh. Then, a thin sliver
behind the roof tops,
its silver smile twittering with accented birds,
ink-blue heightening into paler bloodless white:
daybreak left us exhausted, electric, needing sleep.
I'm twenty, remember. I know nothing.
(Later we arrive at a house owned by the parents

of the other couple in the car. We'll walk next to low, grey
        surf thumping a pebble beach,
we'll fossick shells, sculpted driftwood, nuggets of amber.)
There's a whole afternoon of North Sea sharpening the air
and, for a while, two people's magnetism, guessing each
        other's thoughts,
reading each other's minds. It's like a chess game.
Every move's been planned beforehand,
yet every act of sympathy turns into new surprise.
Each second, time seems beyond movement:
so, stillness releases its leaf-edged play of shining flares.
I know nothing, unable to identify this fear of loss.
Hankering, too, renews its own shadow, its opportunity.
We can go anywhere, be anywhere. We'll make out.
Of course, night will come haunted by midges, surf-noise,
        owls.
Night will bring its windswept silence, too, its haunted
        longing.
But now, there's the way appearing and disappearing merge
        together,
seeming to be one in young acts of love. It's the self losing
        itself,
turned into fire, turned into fear, by sex and beauty.
For a while the self becomes them – fire, fear, sex, beauty,
        that is –
in their unconscious frame: each move's a ladder, out
        nowhere, floating.

KEVIN HART

THE WORD

Say *wood* and everything is clean again.
The word is all around you, like the night,
Impossible to grasp. Your mouth is dark.

A splinter found its way into your quick.
That old tree slit by lightning won't be moved.
Last year's thin rain froze hard inside a trunk

And now a honey flesh shines through cracked bark.
Your mouth is dark. Go far into yourself,
Let quietness gather there, then say the word.

Space

PHILIP HARVEY

NON-CORE PROMISE

The either or toward election dates,
the lowcall member hoardworking hypocritter,
his sunny daisposition, disfunction centred
as the beast of them, the dignified choice
banishing Twaddledeep to the wildernice.
Betwin laborights, a syrup of it's time,
rapresetnaive of the working drinking man
err woman. Whatching the merginalls.
A fare day's work for a fair pay's day.
Remember the november rememberers
envying towards Jerusalem, cartuning faces,
republicising the future. And the coillusion
upending the anti, prophets of the capitalissimo
and his army of stock caractors, big iffers
smooth as a backyarn swimming pool.
How to turn the words into gestures, parsing
liperal sirface while it's business as useyouall.
I can seeze tomirror in tosdays of yer
blahsts the banner in issuespeak.
Whose middle is out classed these terms?
Values slip away from a sound bite, yank
into wholesale commentary half-truths;
minder parties the while pander to facts.
The huffnpuff speaktacle temperratedures

into its last gasp week. Their cartoon phases.
Down the old school grade two Settleday
compulsive vetoers take their cards of boxes:
how to score a dinkey vote. Own, due, twee.
Only whose fortune is really at stake smells
under the closed door of thud ejection night.

Blue Dog: Australian Poetry

Dominique Hecq

LABYRINTH

Steps for nothing.
The alert feeling of a dream — ARAGON

In the caves at Lascaux last century, footprints
of children were found untouched for thousands of years.

Bison, horses and bulls now frozen along
the tortuous passageways of this maze stare

as your step twists into the cave of Three Brothers
where this horned, half-human figure appears.

No one knows who led the children through – what desire
kindled the Magdalenian art of the last ice age.

Could Daedalus and the Minotaur refigure
images of half-man and bull in mere chthonic

chambers as if you could come to know this amazing
cavity hollowed out of time blindfolded?

Plato's narrative of the cave, after all, marks
the ignition of desire in Western thought

for all dank, dark, or tangled metaphor to die
and rise again in the light of rational truth.

As a kid in Bilbao, I recall scuttling through
the back streets looking for my brothers. Being stopped

from taking a short cut. Retracing my steps.
Seeing my first dead body – a bull, three feet away.

Could it be that metaphors form the bones
of language, yet mean nothing beyond their literal

assertions? No Minotaurs. Just monsters marauding
desire. This timeless labyrinth, your inner ear.

Still. The passages of our time show more than enough
half-human creatures posted at every turn, creeping

past mounds of corpses to let go of Ariadne's thread.
The question is whether it is leading out, or in.

Island

JUDY JOHNSON

AT THE TEMPLE OF SISTERS

(*For Kay*)

You ask me to decipher its meaning.
You were alone in the dream, imprisoned with trees.

I quote Li Po, something about the autumn moon
raking white bones – such poise – as if language

had found a way to walk
through the forest of self.

I too am full of dreams.
That you and I lived in a house

with many chambers: ramparts, secret boltholes.

When I woke
your phantom pulse rapped at my temples,

and I reached for those two ten-cent-pieces
of membranous skin on either side of my head

where bone refuses to grow.

I sealed with a finger
whatever was trapped inside

and remembered reading how,

in order to draw out the Devil,
medieval priests held dog's blood

to the temples
in copper chalices.

But snares and exorcisms don't work.

There is nothing to offer your cancer
that it doesn't already have.

And we were never ones for prayer, anyway
except

you told me once
when your children were small

you traced the whirlpools of hair
at those diminutive entry points

to the brain as they slept
and the yielding beneath the surface

seemed to spiral down
through their toes into earth

like the roots of some insatiable oak.
You felt like God, you said,

your finger on the soft-leaf pulse
at the centre of things.

While branches scratched
the window outside

and on the wall

your body's shadow,

enticed through portals
of lamplight,

turned monstrous.

Blue Dog: Australian Poetry

JEAN KENT

TRAVELLING WITH THE WRONG PHRASE BOOKS

(*For Martin*)

LAST DAYS ON OUR USUAL LITTORAL

Sunset into the shipwrecked house tracks spiders' glittering
    seams.
The quilted air pads lightly round us this winter

as we pack and prepare for farewells. I almost forget this
    peninsula
we have beached on, this tongue of land with its lazy phrases
of house and garden, its exclamations of jetties over a lake.

But now, when all our surfaces have been tableclothed
with maps and passports, bills and wills, as I go out into the
    neighbourhood

I hear the Esperanto of end-of-winter walkers ahead of me.
Three men by the bottle shop clutch their beer. In seeding
    grass nearby,
seven magpies just as eagerly sipping. A woman hurtles over
    the hill,

about to take off in pink lycra – and cockatoos & rainbow
    lorikeets flap up,
screeching news of foreign invasion: 'A *flamingo* at Lake
    Macquarie!'

Below our house, the water is calm with cloud. Over this
    mute surface,
swallows flash – then swoop around me as if I could be
    stitched here,
appliquéd forever into this space. I skip place names

over my mind and watch them sink: England – Scotland;
Germany – Lithuania; Queensland Canberra New South
    Wales . . .

We have imagined ourselves all around the planet so much
how can we believe this is where we belong? As the scars of
    the day

are smoothed over, as the water waits for mullet underneath
to leap up neat as needles, restitching a doona big enough
for all the landscapes of our lives to sleep under,

the edge of this world is littered with memories of its history:
sponges of thongs and mussels; chips of coal and amber-
    shimmering
beer-bottle glass . . . Through a rip in the sky, sun slips to
    claim them

and immediately out from under jetties
swallows are swooping, threading themselves with light and
looping it,

from land to water and back – so many webs which should
hold us
to this littoral – so many lines of connection
and abandonment . . . streamering me now like an ocean liner

as I turn to leave, the hulls of my shoes collecting
a last home-crunch.

ON THE PLANE TO PARIS

On the plane to Paris, is it too late to learn French?
The child of migrants – and now a global adult –
you don't think so. *Un deux trois* . . .
merci, merci . . . s'il vous plaît . . .

Confident as a cockatoo, you sprout these comical crests
while I wonder: speechless for six months,
what mercy could you beg for?

War spun your parents' globe and slid them
down to the end of the ocean. You grew up on their island,
lapped by three tongues. Feel quite at home now
with none of them.

So, as yet another culture threatens to swamp you,
only at the last moment do you peg your nose,
try for three minutes to take the senseless plunge . . .

Too late, our seatbelts clicked, Australia beneath us –
all around you suddenly you sense
an embryonic lap, a language before thought,
easy as baby talk and bubbling toward the sky

because yes, this jumbo belly is full of Germans, hungering
home.
The Lufthansa hostess after a quick identi-kit scan
guesses you'll speak her language –
Und 'Ja, danke schön', you do.

Those other sounds which snorted out of you are gone
like blue-bottle pops. Saliva runs over their stings
as you burst the foil round your pretzel, close the lesson
with a sniff. Well, isn't the whole world multi-cultural now?

The plane, at any rate, speaks universally.
Screeching louder than the cockatoos
unfed in our garden tonight,
it launches us into limbo . . .

while I rehearse new ripples
introducing us at our far-off touchdown –

the hostess pearls pure nonsense three different
        ways
into the displaced oyster shells of my ears –

and you   go up into clouds
as calm as the bubbles in your beer
trancing into Tract 1 in the Guide Book
for Word 6   safely settled in our laptop.

AT PHOTO STATION, BOULEVARD ST-MICHEL

What language does it need, the cheeky bird
which is this Photo Station's logo? At home in Ad-Land,
flying under a rainbow and sticking its beak
through a camera lens, it welcomes us.

Snapped for the album now, we'd be forever on this footpath,
glad-mouthed as Christmas bells. But while I'm ringing
with mind-music of *pellicules* and *négatifs,*
the ropes which keep this commerce chiming
turn your tongue to felt. This language love pre-dates us:

a cobble throw from the Sorbonne, it takes me back
to sandstone and gargoyles at St Lucia –
to grit in my mouth and the scowl of cigar smoke
in a tutorial where, to be seventeen and shy and female,
stranded me strange as a bellbird in Quasimodo's ear.

'Today we will discuss *L'Étranger* – the alienation
of Camus – ' *Aah oui,* agrees the tutor's djellabah
of young men, pleating their voices earnestly
around him, *we will, we will.*

In my Pierre Cardin/Vogue Pattern dress,
I am bare-shouldered, shivering in the heat and silence
of Algeria – as I hear the French, the French I thought
I slept in like a stream,

slither over sand, a sinister ripple
no longer to be trusted.

That was 1969. The Paris pavements
had already been overturned. At lunchtime forums
under poincianas in the Brisbane swelter, while pamphlets
printed *Apathy and People's Power* in roneo ink
on our not-yet met fingers

across the Great Court in his laboratory
your Lithuanian father was safely translating symbols
for catalysts, warning of the dangers of Communists,
        forgetting
his student nickname *'Bon ami'.* Your mother,
under lorikeets at Mt Coot-tha was at home,
cooking in German.

Their shadows were not there
in that stifled room. But today on the Boulevard St-Michel,
spelling in French our shared Anglicised name,

mouthing beside you sounds as odd
as formulae for a bomb –

as a narcissus-pale girl in this Photo Station
reels before my Antipodean breath,
                              over all of us
the pall of difference falls. I hear how any tongue
flung into foreign air can strike, reptilian –

while our thoughts are still
kind chimes in our clanging heads.

Westerly

ANDY KISSANE

VISITING MELBOURNE

And then they called out your names
– 'Patchwork Quilt', SWEET HONEY IN THE ROCK

1

I stop. Someone has called my name with
certainty and conviction. My birth
name, not the shortened version I now use.
How did he pick me out from the crowd
on Jolimont station? An eye for faces perhaps,
for the youthful grin lurking in my weathered chin.
An old school mate, excited to see me
after twenty-five years. And I him. My team

had beaten his, once again, but there's
no stirring now, nor any need to brag of goals
bagged from the boundary line. Instead, inevitably,
we talk of those we've seen, or still see, those
who have made it and, as rumour has it,
those who have died by their own hand.

2

Those who have died by their own hand.
The night air so cold we watch each other

breathe. Not completely surprising, but still
there's the shock of knowing someone
who wanted to die more than they wanted
to live. An outsider, an enigma, as we
all are, by degrees. No point shaking heads
or searching for words to make it easy.

Comfort comes most readily in the bright,
blue eyes of his own daughter, standing there
with a black and white scarf wrapped securely
around her neck. Or the photo of my girl
beaming from the window in my wallet.
May that never happen to our own pretty ones.

3

May that never happen to our own pretty ones.
Though they will grow old, as my parents have.
There's no way to avoid it. But at least our
children won't spend these precious years
learning to fire an AK-47, or grieving
for a brother whose unlucky, unsuspecting
foot kicked at an innocent patch of dried mud.
My daughter switches off Grandpa's football

on the radio, then turns on the TV. Told
not to, she does it again and Grandpa
slaps her across the back of the legs. Only
takes a moment, but the imprint of an angry

hand will burn on in our minds like
the orange and violet flash of an exploding mine.

4

The orange and violet flash of an exploding mine
would not even register in my father's occluded
right eye. He can see only darkness –
the result of a routine operation gone wrong.
He gazes at me out of his one good eye
like he does not know me, like I am
a stranger, not his beloved son. My daughter
needs to learn obedience, he says. He means

respect, I guess, that way of making others
feel relaxed, at home. If I talk any more,
I will surely say things I will regret,
I will tell him he just doesn't get it.
Yet even the blind Tiresias senses
the rider clinging to the bolting horse.

5

The rider clinging to the bolting horse
is my niece, Emma. But that's another story.
Horse mad, like my daughter, she drives us out
to the hunt club where her horse, Puzzle,
is recovering from a strained ligament.
We walk through the fields searching

for a quiet pony with a white blaze. He takes
the carrot in one gulp, then sniffs our pockets

for another. Soon my daughter is trotting
around the dressage ring, the pony's hooves
kicking up grey sand. Her back straight, rising
and falling, she smiles each time she passes me.
There's no point denying it, this feeling of
a hand opening up my flesh to graze my heart.

6

A hand opening up my flesh to graze my heart?
Whose hand? Whose heart? Some people
think that there isn't any self to speak of,
no rich inner life. Only stories borrowed
and stolen from others. Like the lines
of this poem, this diminished thing, remade
by fingers that can only grip a pen, sung
by lungs that never pause to think of breathing.

In *Collected Works*, that great Melbourne bookshop
of poetry and ideas, Kris tells me of his son's death
and how he now keeps going by coming in to work.
It's the routine that helps him grieve. Although
I'm surrounded by books stacked to the ceiling,
I mumble something pathetic; I don't know what to say.

7

I mumble something pathetic; I don't know what to say
to my parents. They want me to take some memento
from the family home, before it's sold, something
precious. But all I need is already inside me.
I'll have whatever Greg wants, I say, on purpose,
just to be difficult. The ship with billowing sails,
the brass fire-screen, the china dinner set locked
safely away in the crystal cabinet. At the airport

we hug goodbye, though there are many things
we don't say. Or can't. In the taxi I think
only of you, my week of sole parenting
now done with. Home again, the rain soaks
my hair, my fingers fumble with the keys, then
I stop. Someone is calling my name.

Griffith Review

ANTHONY LAWRENCE

EQUATION

The kookaburra begets the sacred kingfisher
who begets the rainbow bee-eater
who begets the firetailed finch
who begets the forty-spotted pardalote
who begets the damsel fly
who begets the jewelled beetle
who begets a pentangle of reflected light
that falls on a colony of dust mites
who beget particles of skin
blown from a hand in a moment of wonder
at the hard beauty of mathematics
or more precisely the language used to define it
as when a bubble tree mutates into something
indivisible like the tail-end
of the mating call of a powerful owl
driven to the margins of fields
night-vision can take in
until the dead and the soon-to-be-taken
have been filed away inside
your windy demographic
until you have what you think you need
which is anything you desire and more
provided your assessments
are based on the knowledge that living

creatures have no correct lineage

when it comes to this

making of phrase and fable this

learning how to arrive and be prayerful and leave

Australian Book Review

Emma Lew

FINISHING SCHOOL

I know that my pupil is imperfect.
It may be that herein lies her strength.
Small hands, dark eyes – evidence of a passionate nature.
Sure enough, the foot is deformed.

Her eyes are deep, like a pond of black water.
She knows very well how to burrow in the darkness.
It is bitterness I want to teach her –
of which life is woven, the wild bible.

Sweet dreams, delusive hopes.
The taint is passed on from parent to child.
How could anyone as pale as she, I wonder, sit so silently?
I'll never tire of punishing her.

Heat

KATE LLEWELLYN

TONGUE

The tongue is the ego's horse
all muscle and fluid movement
licker of plates spoons and vanities.

On good days my tongue
would like to emulate some of those
National Steeplechase winners
Oscar Wilde for instance
and Dr. Johnson
or those Olympians of dressage
Sarah Bernhardt, Judi Dench
or Zoe Caldwell.
Instead, an oats bag of excuses
hanging from its neck
it idles all day in this orchard
slyly when least expected
kicking out at reputations.
On other days, bold and lithe
it leaps fences,
almost understands mysteries

and returns to its daily hay
munching with satisfaction
yet vaguely ashamed.

Southerly

Kathryn Lomer

SORROW OF THE WOMEN

The sorrow of the women of Hunan province
is written in a script only they can read.
In lines five to seven syllables long
they inscribe their pain like a tattoo
on the calm skin of rice paper,
their own skin bruise-purple or red from rough work.
It is a transparent wrapper for their hurt,
scrolled and sent to sisters, girl cousins, mothers:
the old teach the young.
In this secret code they transform woes
into lines of poetry,
a mosquito scrawl of menstrual blood,
invisible ink of tears
wept for the destiny of women.
Most write no Chinese, have never learned
woman plus woman equals quarrel,
or man plus man plus man is a crowd.
They do know that sun and moon make bright
but someone has taken the sun and moon away.
They pick out words like pictures – mountain, river, field –
and wish all things in their world simple,
but how do you draw a girl taken from her family
or hips too young for childbirth?
Theirs is a syllabary like Cypriot or kana;

they make sloping strokes and curves like women's bodies,
life drawings aslant, awry,
fluent in sorrow, without punctuation.
Or they embroider cushions with silk stitches
in such a way men think them decoration,
the gentle art practised for their comfort.
Subversion comes in many forms,
folded into fans and parasols,
hemmed in, sent beyond lives lived in shadow.
This script is women's business,
a Rosetta Stone of the heart,
love found only between the lines –
the love of this woman writing
for that woman reading.

Space

KATE MIDDLETON

AFTERMATH (GRIEF)

(from 'The Juniper Quartet')

'A month passed and the snow melted.'
Simple words, so often –
the gentle bridge of joy linking one month to the next,
nine months in all, the passing season of marriage.

It is said swans sing before death.
We all sing, the last bubbles of spittle and resignation
an aria of sighs. Snow melts underfoot,
it melts and vapour rises to heaven.

They say ten animals rose, among them
the ram which saved Isaac. My wife rose too,
diminishing as the snow diminished,
the snow's complexion kissing the face of the resurrected.

I married again. A naked mattress
such a sad thing. Vengeance is a language,
sharp cries we all learn, the bloody entwinement of years.
Some time later, a month passed and the snow melted.

The Weekend Australian

PETER MINTER

SERINE

The night wind is over.
  Cold air running over flint leaves
& grey steel fields

white nimbus
  breaking moonlight on hilltops
at bright speed

the clatter of rib bones
  tied to a wheel
spinning under a dark tree

light from a star
  left older than you, its crescent glint.
Seed pods

school in the dark tree,
  a winter shoal,
stay very still beside your window.

Still enough to wake you.
  Closer now, the sky's separation.
They harvest the future

electricity from air, know
  the sun binds
each wafer wing less so

each day to the centre,
  all the light dry
to a core of beginning.

Later in the day,
  a grey cavern over the city
reminds you

that things can fall apart,
  the grass carriage of skins everywhere &
small hard kernels on the path

mend the mind to simple equations
  like, falling away
from the air & going into the ground,

such clockwork in all this.
  Though, one or two pods
blown whole in the night

will never split.
  You take them in. Held to your heart
& the glass

where the tree rushes
  your eye makes a karyotype of dark seeds,
translucent skin.

It's then your face
  close by in the ground
remembers how you have lived.

Island

DAVID MUSGRAVE

YOUNG MONTAIGNE GOES RIDING

Que scais-je?

I wake up to the sound of music played
on pipe or strings – my father's whim, not mine.
He believes my tender brain might bruise
if I wake too suddenly. Saturnine
cows orbit his estate and confuse
themselves with a grove's piebald shade.

It's early. Bullish nostrils quivering steam.
Dew-shuddering trees and a clatter of stallions.
Stuttering chickens peck and servants scrub
floors, an armada of grey galleons
scouring shallows. One of them, a snub-
nosed woman, I recall – that is, I seem

to recall, for I have no memory to speak
of, only curiosity – comes from the same
village on my father's estate where I
was put out to nurse. I greet her by name.
Mornings like these, before the sun gets high,
I like to ride: I prefer the oblique

paths which wander and meander to the one
which goes straight to the truth. Mist rises
from the fields, all patchwork, like our deeds,
and we ride. How one exercises
one's judgement choosing a suitable steed
is a question worthy of a theologian:

do we judge a horse racing, walking or at rest
in the stable? And how do we judge a king:
upon the throne of state, or on that private
throne, his private estate? I read the steaming
dollops falling from the jouncing nates
of my companion's horse as I would a text

of some thousands of words, theorising
on the consistency of excrement
and what it tells us of the teeth, the heart,
the firmness of the gut and the contentment
and the clearness of a conscience. The fart
is a different matter: a vapid, rank uprising

disproving the obedience of the anus
as it is discussed in Vives' commentary
on Augustine's man who synchronised
his farts to the steady alimentary
metre of verses his friends devised.
Usually it is most unruly and mutinous –

much like our current form of government.
I am fortunate to be born in depraved times:
for very little effort I am thought
virtuous; abstaining from the crimes
which are the weapons of that war fought
here, in the hub of civil discontent,

allows me idle hours, time which breeds
chimeras and grotesque things. Variety
alone satisfies me. We pass a field
of sheaves of wheat whispering like a society
of academicians. Weighed down by their yield
they learn humility and lower their heads,

but in the next field ears of wheat rise high
and lofty, heads erect and proud as they
are empty. What do I know? That I can't bear
being shut up in a room, that children play
with knucklebones, men with words, and where,
before they enter our lives, diseases lie

is a mystery? Silent veins of smoke
thread the air. Over the fields a clump
of houses appears, bristling with sound: notes
from a strident rooster, the mill's slow thump.
This is the village where children suckle on goats
and the poor hide their diseases with a cloak

of gentle words which relieve the pain and soften
their harshness. What would we do without names?
Worldly troubles are mostly grammatical
and we have taught our ladies' cheeks to flame
at the mere mention of what they are not at all
afraid to do. Sometimes in daylight. And often.

I could ride for hours: pacing does not tire
me as much as a set journey which forces
me straight ahead instead of the roads which chance
throws up. I think my ideas are like horses.
Sometimes they follow each other at a distance;
at others they glance sidelong at each other.

The path declines and we descend and muddy
hooves spatter our caparisons.
To what could I liken this river? A moulting
snake? What matter our comparisons
when this river, like a civil war, is revolting
against itself, eroding its banks? I study

the surface, shedding scales of light; beneath,
on the river-bed the wind's shadow furrows
its skin like a plough. I study everything:
what I must flee and that which I must follow,
although since my earliest days nothing
has occupied my mind more than death,

but I've never gnawed my nails over Aristotle.
Once, as I stood on the headland of my brother,
the Sieur d'Asac's lands in Médoc I saw the waves
break over what was once his land. At another
time he had been rich: now, nothing save
fens and drains remain from his battle

with the sea. We continue over dunes
under puffed up clouds and pass a flotilla
of ducks quacking in tiny epicycles
on the current. I cannot stay still. A
mind does nothing but whirl around like little
silkworms which then get tangled in cocoons.

One and the same pace of my horse seems to me
now rough, now easy; the same road at one
time shorter, another time longer; one and the same
view now more, now less pleasing; the sun
now shines too hot, now too feeble a flame
to warm my tired bones. Now I am ready

to do anything, now to do nothing. I do
nothing but come and go and I'm unable
even to rid myself of vice, I just exchange
one for another. Only a fool is immovable
and certain. The sun has become a blazing orange
rising towards the meridian of depthless blue.

It's getting hot. I could stay all day
in the saddle, riding around and about without
flagging. Recently I've heard of a tribe
of cannibals in the new world. I do not doubt
there is more barbarity in eating a man alive
than dead; but who are we to talk, who flay

our enemies alive like dumb creatures
when they are men, like us? These cannibals
know valour; they would rather be killed and eaten
than ask not to be. To a man they are unable
to yield to fear: they are killed, not beaten.
But then again, they do not wear breeches.

A horn sounds. My neighbour hunts again.
Gentlemen are mounting their horses, eager
to course across the grounds and chase some hare,
petrified, and watch lean hounds crush meagre
bones and fur in their grim jaws. I share
the thrill of a hunt, but cannot stand the pain.

I steer my horse homewards – there is a shelf
in my circular library filled with books which say
the earth and planets revolve around the sun.
Perhaps that is the case. For every day
our fortunes change and turn around our sovereign
king. But I revolve within myself.

JASON NELSON

HOW THE SUN WORKS

From a distance, somewhere between two
and a half million miles and seventeen inches, I look
sad. It's not my fault, but rather the gnomes
living on my face. They're tiny creatures,

with hairy foreheads and three big stubby fingers.
They operate a series of pulleys and a lattice work
of scaffolding around my mouth. You can't see
them. No, not even if you had an electron microscope

and a Norwegian lab assistant, could you see
their fumbling hands yanking and contorting
my expressions. You have to understand
it's really not my fault that I look sad. Somewhere

deep in the bureaucratic mess of gnome society
it is required by gnome law that I look sorrowful
and distraught. I've tried legal manoeuvres, but I'd need
knee pads and really loose hip sockets, which are expensive

and messy. I've hired a lobbyist for the next gnome
legislative session, in hopes of at least changing
the law enough so I can go from looking sad
to just looking slightly confused.

_____

Meanjin

John Nijjem

AT TURIN

It would have all been better had Nietzsche taken residence
in Ronda or in Akragas or became a strict recluse on one of
     the Aeolians. He thought
Tuscany a place of health but himself lived mostly
     Schopenhauerian, pausing
in small rooms, haunting northern spaces. It's legend now, his
     embracing at Turin
of the horse. The carriage driver might have felt ashamed at
     his own cruelty, then
disgust at the impertinent sentimentality of that sickly looking
     foreigner so removed
from the world, who could not bear the way pain accrues
to the image of things; who could not accept the human work
     of pain
as ordinary.

     To see a madman rushing towards him, inarticulate,
          blubbering, cleaving
to the sweaty neck; compelled and exorbitant . . . The beast in
     any case was blind,
so many times that thick whip had stung across its open eyes
     (though not intentionally).
But the way it was inured to its suffering, that it had long been

pastured with blows – *did you see that also*? It was no longer there
as it appeared to be there; unabated cruelty has its own
peculiar mercy.

Not just the giving but the surviving of pain requires a
    certain degree
of stupidity, in most creatures at least. Stupidity, of course,
    may have a
force and elegance –
a meticulousness; the prophylaxes of representation – the
    world construed
as *Vorstellung*, the gaze as neurosis. The truly sound person is
appropriately unhappy, blunts the ability to see too well since
    what is pain
but awareness? To see too well's of no benefit to us. The parts
    of us
that suffer most are dark. *You* knew this. You *knew* this. But
    what in us cannot help us?

―――――――――――――――――――

Meanjin

JAN OWEN

THROUGH KERSENMARKT

Maastricht

Five Slavs in black and red are strumming up fire,
flaunting their tambourines – the ribbons, the dips of song!
It buoys you over St Servaas Bridge to the deaf-mute girl
safe on her low stool, plucking an earlier music from the air;
left, right, left, her finger cymbals
lodge shut mantras in your ear,
as on and on her smile keeps time in the June sun.
No spring of finger from thumb lets metal sing
its silver intimations of thought,
each beat gulps its resonance down,
cause and effect turned dumb.
All day the flat clap trap of her left hand echoes her right;
for counterpoint – the ring of a coin or two in her tin
as the feet and bicycles pass.
Her face is landscape clear to the skyline, clear to the source.
All day the long dark barges slide down-river
under her bridge and on.

Blast Magazine

Dorothy Porter

WATERVIEW STREET

In the street
of my childhood
nothing is reliable.

My parents' friends are dead.
Their children gone.
Familiar houses
are dissolving.

I'd welcome the macabre
solid comfort
of cemeteries and weeds
but instead
there is a tropical
rotting splendour
that disturbs and distracts
like an invisible cockatoo
shrieking from a tree.

Time is melting
everything I remember
into a soft silt
shifting under the mud-mangrove
smell of the bay.

While I wait
for the eternally salty water
to unanchor all my memories
and sweep my old self away.

Australian Book Review

PETER PORTER

THE LAST GRUPPETTI

There is no such thing as maturity.
Wagner writes stiff Weberian tunes,
stiffer far than Weber's, but the best
employ those signal little turns,
gruppetti, helping raise his melodies
to some redemptive ecstasy,
genuflecting as they go.

The idiocies of our childhoods resurrect
as fantasies gathering on the shores
of death. If we stepped into a sealed train
it would not deliver us from the plague-filled town.
The fear which stood on wet verandahs once
gestures as a Bessarabian Ice-Cream Vendor
grinning behind his farting horse.

But welcome to Transfiguration.
You won't arrive at Monsalvat unless
You're on a lifetime's pilgrimage. Brass
and clarinet are striding on the crutches
of chromaticism. Along the path down which

the dove descended, *gruppetti* turn their backs
on the Winter Landscape and enter Heaven.

Australian Book Review

PETER ROSE

BEACH BURIAL

(For Craig Sherborne)

Grief wrongs us so — DOUGLAS DUNN

To the sea we bear our fathers in state –
or what they've done to them: the square conversions.
Surf mild as receding tides,
we slump in dunes with our burdens,
our careful, ignored speeches.
No one notices what's borne in a casket,
old sumpture furnaced in the drabbest stove,
death a utilitarian blast.
But surprisingly heavy, refractory,
so that we have to retrace our footsteps
and find something (a knife even)
to hack it open with –
so violent we almost attract
attention in those dunes. Almost.
No one heeds the deepening night
or what's being plundered.
You swim among them with those ashes,
unknown, isolate, unforgiven.
Not even our fathers listen to those last
hoarse gasps of regret and acknowledgment:
whether poem or lied or code or rant.

Like becalmed fishermen
or last tentative swimmers
or octogenarians tugging rinsed Pomeranians,
our fathers are preoccupied,
turn their heads west – even in death.

Australian Book Review

GIG RYAN

KANGAROO AND EMU

1

He surveys the tilled electorate, covets
his faded abacus of watched commentators
hauled jockeys who don't know what's missed
The record leader gnaws his record to the core
family smote around him in a lei
'We stick with what we know'
says the marginalled, marshalling her TV bytes
a bodyguard of season's values and the stressed deputy
tiddlywink attentively

2

'Excitement for the first time in yonks' a struck gallery keys
as the new leader estimates the stage
His kids circuit the maths chairs
An ex sighs

Aspirations whine like a semaphore
when popularity slated its
gift selves from the Tree of . . .

'We have signed niiine memoranda' the minister umpteenths out
ramping up his slush fund's rumpled horn

or promise to change Tuesday to Monday
pulling a lizard from a hat

a ring of certainty buttered on his finger
raffling through a sulk, a ute
a nodule sheared off by his mates

3

Swaggering misanthrope marooned in a nib
you go through the liege bracelet
and plethora friends living in their own coinages and scam

> '*We decide who comes into this country*'
> by algorithm or parachute
> '*and the circumstances in which they come*'

with always the assumption that anywhere is better
crimson paddock and peppercorn or clattered heath he can't
    beguile
a punter of woe riding out of luck.

_____

Heat

PHILIP SALOM

---

sections from THE MAN WITH A
SHATTERED WORLD

*A palimpsest on the story of Zasetsky, brain-damaged in WWII, and his
attempts to recover from chronic aphasia, observed by his physician
A. R. Luria, the Russian neurologist.*

Face-down in Id
shellshock
mudwound
generalanaesthesia
patronymic dreamsof
sexanddeath

as they lift you from   your ditch of star-shells
your eyes a crocodile's   opening from the mud

the light is migraine   the world is flat where
your name was   clouds of smudge

when you lift your head   from the pillow
the hospital glare   overwhelming overlit

as heaven the wards   crowded with the risen
from where   dead as deep water the

poem of evermore begins   and eats you
stanza by stanza   from mud into mudlight

* * *

Being shot in his left temporal parietal lobes
ruined his right side of everything – a cat-like pupil
pounds like a splinter in his brain:

the images a needle in a groove
should play back crooning
its love of the world . . . but his universe
recedes by half of everything
and half of every half is infinity
like a metaphysical conundrum

as the tilting halves
of the township are watching
as the women at home   are watching
he sees half of a full head of cabbage
on the table in front of him
then half of that leaf then
half a crease . . .

watching the physicians leaning forwards in their seats
as he stands nakedly before them:
like Rembrandt's The Anatomy Lesson, the scalpel
and the colours of seriousness

above dissection of the corpse . . .
he is some kind of *criminal*?

Pedagogues, scientists, reductionists,
he is halved: his own sight
sections everything
       (the physicians are)
       (sicians a)
       (cia)
       (i)

           * * *

He grips the pencil
like an etching tool
to make each sentence
score the surface so
deeply each letter
goes down up into
the blink-sheet of his
left brain, the dark.
Every day he forgets
and starts again.

Who could blame him
falling down drunk in the street
the words burning his stomach
in farmyard fury, trapped, each

hobble and joint pain
a wrecked syntax.

For twenty five years
trying to wake up free of it
the world in one place
the words filling into him
like champagne and listen
to them moved to tears

words which give him back and strip him
as he stares at the pixelating
blackboard.

* * *

Seeing is a fern in the brain
where the world still drips and whistles.
The eye shapes us, our three
dimensions   the urge to copulate.

If he has a lover, if,
then just to see her he must scan
back and forth as if shaking his head.

He stares through the window at cars.
He is a cat, the pupil's black line.

There's truth to conjugate: If an elephant is
bigger than a tank, is a 20 year old soldier . . .?

'Perhaps they took my brain out
altogether. Or cut the left side off
and put it back in again. I dream.
I can imagine with my right. I am
a little brain left out in the snow.'

At night the air is cold
across the valley, a diesel
beats like a slow repeating gun
under the stars.
Looking up he almost
tastes the tang of constants
the black roof of his brain
scattered with salt.
The sky is heavy
as the Russian language.
He   its smallest
black hole
its beating
syllable
I

Westerly

ALEX SKOVRON

SORCERY

What sorcery is this? I need to know. When I touch the
surface of the sphere, my fingers glow. When I imagine the
shapes it morphs into, imaginings flow. When I dream, or day,
or when deflect, it almost opens to me, but vision blurs. When
I awake, endeavour to reclaim, nothing occurs. The meaning of
the shapes is meaning, I would capture it, but cannot catch. The
purpose of the surfaces is purpose, I try to skim across, but can-
not snatch. It magics at me when I step the street, it wizards in
me when I come to sleep. It is the simplest riddle in the world, I
am possessed. It is the puzzle most profound, I cannot rest. My
eyes can close, within the blackness it bewitches me. My eyes
reopen, swallow light, the dark enriches me. I face my glass, it
shimmers when I dress, cannot discard it. I turn away, return to
nakedness, the conjurors guard it. Do you divine, I ask them,
what I feel? No answer pushes past them. What is real? When
words abandon me, I shiver, try to sing. The song puts back the
words my questions bring. The dreams bring back the song,
the song I know. When I touch the surface of the song, my
fingers glow. They trace the shape, seeking the mystic skin, but
nothing's there. One day, one day, I'll peel away the sorcery.
If I dare.

Meanjin

KATHLEEN STEWART

HOW I GOT AWAY

My horse's name was Fear
How fiercely white and black
his ermine mane and how precise
the steps he took as down we rode
the shell spiral of the tower
The rush of his hooves
as we tumbled forward
bright as Lucifer in his fall
down and down the light shafts
first the ivory tower and then
the long horizon of the ebony
shying at the portals of mercy and severity

My horse's hooves were brutal on the earth
We were pursued by their echoes
as if followed by a horde of
ghost horses, who bared their teeth
and struck their hooves upon the ground
and split open a way of darkness
Even now the pounding
as the past gives way
the beat of days mounded upon days

I saw a grassy plain
the grass so high
and dressed with shining daisies
I saw a frozen lake
and felt my brittled heart crack
with empathy for its still state
How the lake opened to me
with what sighs
so that the startled swans flew upward

I kissed my horse
and left my blood-prints on his mane
I plunged my hands into the lake
My hands were never mine again

For more than a hundred days we rode
across the fields of snow
As far as the eye could see, ice daisies
What came after me?
Only sorrow
Occasionally I lay down
and waited for it to overtake.

After three hundred and fifty days
my horse stalled
We grazed on sea daisies
countless as the days ahead
and behind
until I saw the ocean rise

Fierce fear rode me on its back
through the floor of the earth into survival
carried me like a child bride
into the roar of life
the waves of all possibilities
tumbling like glassine light.

Meanjin

MARIA TAKOLANDER

STORM

Dreams don't happen like this
Although we think they should,

The earth giving in, flattening
To the darkness, the storm

Fattening, blacking like squid.
It creates its own space,

This *petit mal*, this little night,
With a need as vast as that

Of the beginning of time.
It may be true we don't deserve this,

Our earthly things reduced
To shadows we dream

Things from: the firs, the stooks,
The fence posts – none belong.

They don't belong.
Yet we've always waked and slept

When the sky says we should,
Like birds and monkeys

Abandoning the world,
Evening after evening

With each noiseless revolution,
To the secrets of insects and bats.

Each morning we find
Something changed:

Something added –
A shift in the soil,

The sibilance of grass.
After rain, there are snails,

Startling as hailstones.
But always less remains.

And we're left with this hurting,
As if in the darkness

Or the infant light
We might have seen

The ocean as it really is
Or god.

Australian Book Review

Barbara Temperton

THE LIGHTHOUSE KEEPER'S WIFE

Not an ordinary lighthouse,
her home on the hillside above the channel.
Not an ordinary lighthouse:
a cottage with a double-ridged roof,
south wall bisected by a weather-boarded tower
squared and copper-capped, three keeper-lengths high.

Not an ordinary cottage,
walls as wide as her husband's chest,
the tower-light a maypole the keeper's wife
and daughters skip around west-east, east-west.

Once, she saw a ghost, grey as possibility,
drip salt water along the passageway
some long-drowned former tenant drawn back to trim
the twin wicks, combined bright light visible for miles.

Not an ordinary garden,
She's cultivating granite where the lighthouse stands.
Not an ordinary garden, she's cultivating wind
to harass the keeper's tough-stuff,
growing stunted in kero drums,
through soils he's backpacked in flourbags.
The woman nurtures native rush-grasses in fault-lines,

a reclining melaleuca in the fertile gap between two boulders,
bright lichens as a border between the land and sea.
Not a connoisseur of silence, she's cultivating noise
the sea is never silent here, the nights are never dark.

Working against the keeper is not unlike embroidery
and every time her sense of duty hems her in
the keeper's wife dwells on the night the light went out,
her second daughter's fall into her father's sea;
and her own night-blindness; blundering around on the rock
in her nightdress in the dark and knowing the storm was
    tearing
the whitecaps from the waves, and she was two-times
    bereaved.

Working against the keeper is not unlike embroidery.
With every pass of his magician's needle through the fabric
of the sea, she has a counter-pass with thread:
stem stitch becomes herringbone, blanket stitch chain,
a temporary tack an oversew, and she resets the hoop daily,
straining the weave until the grain is warped.
And she rehearses tangles, French knots, lattice stitch,
keeps her needles shining, her scissor blades sharp.

And just when she thinks she has her husband where she
    wants him,
she stands at the table in the kitchen comparing cottons,
sizing thimbles, tape's capacity to gauge her blackness.

When from this vantage point she detects the keeper
shepherding the channel current east, she turns it west,
when he reroutes the cove rips north, she turns them south,
when he guides a freighter cautiously toward the harbour
she gouges its hull out on a hitherto unknown shoal.

From the light tower the kero drums, performing
their daily cycle of expansion and shrinkage, toll dully.
She knows the smell of kerosene as well
as she knows her own distilled essence,
the scent of her children's hair, the keeper's salty presence.
Kerosene smudges everything with its hazy-blue skin:
is the lighthouse's other tenant, always present, never seen,
a bitter layer on the lips after she's kissed her husband's hand.
And remembering her daughter's dog barking until its voice
    was gone,
she wonders how long she could scream
before she would not make another sound.

_____

Westerly

CHRIS WALLACE-CRABBE

THE ALIGNMENTS

A dot
has only one direction,
a line has two,
or so we were taught at school
back in the short pants and gravel days
long before particle physics.

Tell me, please,
which way
did Time go?
I'd love to know.

And early on
as a child-metaphysician,
my daughter up and queried it all:
'Why do things
have a line around them?'
She ought to have tried Wittgenstein.

Just making it longer and longer, where does it get you?

Looking out over
the ocean's long inhuman reticence,

what rhythmical alternatives,
what miles of diamonds!

Toward orange sunset
on the grass-dry plain
I stare stupidly at silvery railway lines,
thinking they meet near infinity.

Making the slow line dip and sway in its motion
proceeding gravely into and out of the limelight
is worth the endeavour, if you are given to word-games,

which all of us are in one way or another,
playing at words of love and the diction of dying,
what we say being just as green as the world is.

Why is our writing all made up of lines?
There must be something capillary about signs:
look how the envious ink uncoils and twines.

Days of reflective Paul Klee!
It was the painter then
                    talking of
taking a line for a walk, like a dog,
that really set me off
                    on this little track.

Dream of a geometer or some architect's draughtsman,
        the beautiful russet sandstone
has been laying down its hairline strata
        as fine as Thomas Bewick ever did
to capture our attention with lineations:
        engraving in three dimensions!

        Things baffle me,
        solids have turned out so mysterious.
        I think they are the matter
        our dreams were made of,
                                crudely enough
        by smiths and naiads
                        in the Silver Age.

        Following me, old footprints,
        you trace a trail
        across our imagined map,
        mile after dotted mile
        far to the nor'-by-northwest,
        or so it feels to me.

        Evening glides silently in
        to ask us what
        merest reality may be,
        any more than, say,
        lines and shadows,
        shadow and line.

Whatever the headlines
in that dawn-thrown morning paper,
some passing snail
has left its own strand
of autobiography
in calligraphy of silver
there,

         across the doorstep.

      How short
would a life have to be
for sheer disappointment?

      And how very short
the would-be defining line
that was only a dot in space?

Heat

LESLEY WALTER

HYPHENATED LIVES

(*Chang and Eng Bunker, 1811–1874*)

I. BEGINNINGS: MELANGE, SIAM

I cannot turn my back on my brother –
we're fused in front, made to face each other,
can turn our heads only so far. Chang.
Forever in the corner of my eye. We live so close,
our urine often splashes on the other's feet
or slippers. We don't know what it is
to be alone. Pregnant women skirt us
but our mother says she's blessed. We're as nimble
and as quick on our feet as any other, as lithe
in the Mekong as the fish our father catches,
are wont to row his boat for him –
our arms and legs are strong.

II. THE ROAD SHOW

We're Captain Coffin's 'Siamese Double Boys'.
People flock to see us. The freckled ones
with funny eyes and frizzy hair *ooh* at our back-flips,
aah at our battledore. We fly across the ground
like the small cork ball with feathers that we chase
for their entertainment. But later, so many questions!

Yet, what of their own strangeness? We would not trade
our band of skin for such hairy limbs and faces.

III. EXPERIMENTS

Doctors are fascinated – they wonder if
we're really one; not two. They tickle Eng.
I laugh. They prod me in the dead of night.
It is Eng who wakes. They feed me asparagus –
are confounded when Eng's urine doesn't smell.
So, we run our *own* little experiments . . .
Only Eng buys a ticket. And who can lawfully
throw him off a train because his brother doesn't?!

IV. TURNING POINT

Yet since our dual marriage, we try to turn
aside as best we can. But I sense my brother's
hand upon her sex, I hear their bliss; am rocked
by them as though upon a ship. I cannot brace myself
against the tempest – I cannot calm the pounding
of my heart, nor slow or quiet the quickening
of my breath. The darkness that envelops us
is nothing. I'll sometimes slip a hand beneath
the sheet and come, as one, with them. At other
times I wake, my trousers wet. I cannot turn
my back on my brother. I cannot turn my back
upon this woman in our bed. But each morning,
we sip tea together from fine blue china cups.

V. SECRETS

At first, I was shy. When my husband's brother spoke,
I kept my eyes lowered. But I cannot tell the man
I married secrets, without his brother hearing them as well.
They wend their way into his brother's ear, carried via
the blood across shared flesh. I am wedded, now, to both.
But still, it is my husband's seed trickling down
the inside of my leg. Or is it?

VI. SISTERS

We, too, are tied by blood, though not by flesh,
Our bodies spin full circle, separate. Once,
we kept no secrets from each other; but now
I dare not tell her how her husband cups my breasts,
how tenderly he mouths them in the dark.
My brother's hands are deft, the intrigue sweet.
I pity women bedded by one man.

VII. THE ALLURE

Her skin smells of sandalwood, her hair,
of temple flowers. I brush her lips with mine
as she lies slumped across his chest. Her breath's
like clouds of lemongrass and fresh-cut coriander.
I dream again my past; smell again my mother . . .
Brother's wife, wife's sister – sister-in-law
twice over. Surely, then, as near to me as wife.

VIII. QUESTIONS

We do not walk abroad, now, very often.
People turn to look. Not only children point.
It isn't hard to know what they are thinking.
Our cat's tail, too, is a curling question mark.
It asks us who belongs to whom.
We are no longer sure. And does it matter?

IX. THE THIN EDGE

I do not have my husband's ear. Always,
his brother has it. Though even they are come
to blows, what with Chang's penchant for whisky
and Eng's for late-night poker! But they nested
in their mother's womb together; limbs entwined,
breast to breast; pressing ever closer to each other.
And flesh links them, still, like a broad umbilicus.
I thought through carrying children I would better
understand the bond they share. Bone of my bone . . .
flesh of my flesh . . . But no! Every child I grow
is separate. And my sister and I don't speak now –
except for our bickering. Today, she turned her back
on me and simply walked away. It was that easy . . .
For us . . .

X. ENDINGS: NORTH CAROLINA

I'm pinned here in the dark, chilled by his stillness –
can just slip one foot off the edge of the mattress.

I touch the floor's coolness – so different from the marble-
    cold
of him. I sweat; am faint with effort; can barely muster
strength to rouse my son. He goes rushing
through the house sobbing, *Uncle Chang is dead!*
Already I feel numbness in my toes and in my fingers,
my son's voice sounding like the death knell that it is.

Island

MEREDITH WATTISON

IBSEN'S FAWN

He is an Ibsenism.
This orally fixated dog
is voracious.
His mouth
measures
everything.
His gasping, gripping
morning greeting
renders my forearm
teethed, tongued,
known.
He works at all skins
as an anatomist,
sated.
Manoeuvres
a bulb of bone
like a pearl
on a string.
Licks my hands
with sensory zeal,
my feet
like a wild romantic.
His teeth degenerate,
his tongue plebeian.

The plexus of his mouth,
esoteric,
defiling.
All society begins there.

Meanjin

SIMON WEST

I GIORNI DELLA MERLA

And once again the blackbird's days come round,
punctual as moons, while arctic winds pitch
down from the north, and precarious streetlights sway
like silent golden bells above the town.
A little dust moves and gone is the grey lie.
Ice gleams, as if we almost could believe
the miserable swallows tucked under eaves,
or clear between facades of glass the sky.

Nothing will come in place of the blackbird
who holds our thoughts in twists and turns but doesn't
appear. Only the evening falling,
the lonely lights of shop fronts uninviting,
the tired stares of those who await the wasn't
of a century, or the darting shadow of a word.

Famous Reporter

Contributors' Notes

ROBERT ADAMSON lives with his partner, the photographer Juno Gemes, on the Hawkesbury River, New South Wales, where he writes, fishes and draws birds. His highly praised autobiography, *Inside Out*, was published by Text in 2004. His selected poems, *Reading the River*, was published in the UK by Bloodaxe Books in 2004. His latest book of poetry, *The Goldfinches of Baghdad*, was published in the US by Flood Editions in 2006.

Adamson writes: 'I wrote "A Visitation" after a dream that may have originated in a memory of watching wallabies on the Hawkesbury. When I was young, there was a large colony of rock wallabies living on Goat Island (named after the feral goats that could be seen standing on the high escarpments). Although their numbers have been greatly depleted, the wallabies are still living on the shores of the river. The foxes have been poisoned and the goats have been shot. I often see wallabies in the early morning, they appear sometimes as ghostly figures in the mists.

'I thought wallabies on Goat Island, when I first saw them in the 1950s, *were* yellow-footed rock wallabies. This was probably because, at the time, I was poring over John Gould's prints in his *Mammals of Australia*. A lithograph of the yellow-footed rock wallaby had caught my eye – and it was this image that remained as an imaginary presence in my mind until it was transformed into what seemed like a real wallaby by my dream. A yellow-footed rock wallaby. It wasn't until I wrote this poem, that I checked, and discovered the river wallabies weren't yellow-footed rock wallabies at all, they were the more common rock wallabies.

'I wanted the poem to be an open field where the yellow-footed rock wallaby could return to an invented place. As far as we can tell yellow-footed rock wallabies have never lived on the river. However up until recent times it was thought that these wallabies were native to South Australia, but in the mid-1980s yellow-footed rock wallabies were discovered in equal numbers in Queensland. Who is to know that they may once have lived on the Hawkesbury?

'The naturalist Thomas Ward wrote in the early 1880s about the Sydney area: "the Rock-wallaby is by far the most abundant of the animals, and yet it is a much persecuted creature. Rock-wallaby shooting is a favourite sport with all classes of colonists."'

LUKE BEESLEY is a Brisbane writer of poetry and short fiction. His first collection, *Lemon Shark*, was published in early 2006 in the 'soi 3 modern poets' series.

Beesley writes: 'When I wrote "The Fight" I was staying in the Blue Mountains where I was writing for long hours, for consecutive days, between sudden storms; and the writing seemed to be pulling up dreams and little fragments of memory, which I was able to hold well into the morning. I can't throw much light on the meaning, or the specific circumstances. I was thinking about shapes and the alphabet at the time, and there was an image of fighters sparring and making shapes with their bodies in the specific ambience of a kitchen. Really, the poem came to me in one rush and then I didn't look at it again for weeks. It was only coming back to the writing that it seemed to stand out and contain something succinctly odd and dreamy and perhaps mythical to me.'

JUDITH BISHOP is a linguist and lives in Sydney. She was the Marten Bequest Scholar in Poetry for 2002–04, and she gained a Master of Fine Arts in Writing (Poetry) at Washington University in St Louis in 2004. She is currently compiling her first poetry manuscript.

About 'Rabbit' Bishop writes: 'To begin with, there was a real rabbit; but in my poems, there is always a real rabbit, so to speak. I crossed its path, or it crossed mine, one early evening in a park in St Louis, Missouri. Keeping that encounter at its heart, the poem nonetheless evolved into a formal exercise: I was exploring long-lined poems at the time, and the emotional urgency and breathlessness such lines engender; I'd also been reading villanelles and sestinas and was interested in the effects of repeating end-words; and I wanted to write a poem that would be vocative, rather than merely descriptive. Content-wise, in the days before, I'd been absorbing Ted Hughes' and Sylvia Plath's respective *Collected Poems*: their controlled savagery. This rabbit, stretched to its fullest extent in flight (an image crossed with Zeno's arrow), can't run fast enough to save its skin, but tries; and out of that interval, poised between life and death, I wanted to make a trope for our own, vigorous, unattainable sense of our potential, which looks toward the certainty of death.'

STEPHEN EDGAR lives in Sydney. He is the author of six volumes of poetry, the most recent of which is *Other Summers* (Black Pepper, 2006). 'Man on the Moon' was the winner of the inaugural *Australian Book Review* Poetry Prize in 2005.

Edgar writes: 'I don't know that "Man on the Moon" requires much comment. At any rate, there is nothing I wish to say about it except to point out that it is part of a suite of poems, "Consume My Heart Away", and that some readers of the poem in isolation have drawn the erroneous conclusion that it is an elegy for one who has died. This is not the case. Anyone who wishes to read the poem in context will find the whole suite in *Other Summers*.'

DANNY GENTILE lives in Newcastle and works full time writing poetry. He is currently preparing his first book for publication.

Gentile writes: '"The Lenten Veil" is a poem that required little reworking from its original form. It was written straight into the word-processing program of my computer. As with much of my work it was written very quickly, probably taking around half an hour to create. Coming back to it to rework it for submission I changed a few phrases to improve the flow and sense of the work. The title proved more difficult as it was originally included in a suite of poems that had an overall title and were simply numbered. Initially I called it "Ash Wednesday" but was unhappy with the obviousness of this title. The final name came from doing some research on the internet on the Catholic observance of Ash Wednesday and Lent.'

JANE GIBIAN is a Sydney poet whose most recent publication is a chapbook of haiku, *long shadows* (Vagabond Press, 2005). In 2002 she was an Asialink Literature Resident in Hanoi, Vietnam. She works as a librarian, and studies Vietnamese and TESOL.

About 'Ardent' Gibian writes: 'I like being conscious of seasonal changes, and thinking about the passing of time from that angle; both subtle changes and the more obvious ones. In this poem I've taken some particularly Australian signs of such change, like the specific birdcalls made when goannas are hunting for food before autumn in the bush area where I grew up. I've also used other natural phenomena such as the seasonal appearance of flowers. I wanted to merge these concrete images with more dream-like concepts, and so make them less concrete. The poem mixes these elements, and tries to capture a state of emotional overflow; being at the edge of some sort of spilling over.'

KEVIN GILLAM is a West Australian poet, with work published in numerous Australian and overseas journals. His first collection, *Other Gravities*, was published in 2003 by SunLine Press. He is employed as a secondary school music teacher, freelance cellist and part-time creative-writing tutor.

Gillam writes: '"Low at the Edge of the Sands" was written as a dedication to Elizabeth Jolley, one of my first creative-writing lecturers at Curtin University. The title is drawn from one of her short stories, and throughout there are numerous references to both her manner and dress. "Calicoed thievery", for example, refers to both her preference for using a roughly hewn shoulder bag and an alertness for procuring new turns of phrase or slang. The poem then fuses these images/memories with the life of the weedy sea dragon, a relatively exotic species, with a tendency for social isolation.'

ALAN GOULD is a poet, novelist and essayist. His most recent volume of poetry was his *The Past Completes Me, Selected Poems 1973–2003*, and he has completed his seventh novel, provisionally titled *The Seaglass Spiral*, of which several chapters have appeared in Australian journals.

About 'Iris' Gould writes: 'Like many, I feel a resistance to stating a plain position with regard to religious faith. I am neither Anglican nor Atheist. However, I am alive to how marvellous are the patterns of Creation, how mysterious is the question as to whether existence has meaning beyond a brief historical presence. If agnosticism is the mental attitude that best suits my uncertainty on religious matters, then I require this to be a dynamic kind of uncertainty. "Iris" is trying to find its way into a means of religious meditation where the imagination and attentiveness to the world do not become shadowy in assumptions of faith and faith's metaphysics.'

PHILIP HAMMIAL has had nineteen collections of poetry published, two of which were shortlisted for the Kenneth Slessor Prize (in 2001 and 2004). He is also a sculptor with thirty solo exhibitions and the director of The Australian Collection of Outsider Art.

Hammial writes: 'Like many of my poems "Water" was written in a trance, the poem writing itself in four or five minutes. After the fact of its composition, I see that it speaks about The Drought, Australia's biggest future problem (forget Howard's hype about terrorism). There is also a reference to the Mahdi, in this case Muhammad Ahmad al-Mahdi whose dervish soldiers defeated Gordon's troops at Khartoum in 1885. In 1983 I visited a village on the outskirts of Khartoum and was privileged to watch the dervishes dancing out in the desert, 45 degrees and not a breath of air – a pile of shoes and slippers in the middle of a large circle of about one hundred dancing men, some in the self-made green robes of the local order. How the Mahdi made his contribution to Paris (the Avenue Foch) is anyone's guess. Harry Kline, the author of *Paradise Now*, isn't a real author; he's simply a product of my feverish imagination.'

JENNIFER HARRISON is a Melbourne writer and child psychiatrist. She has published three books of poetry and one collaborative collection. She won the 1995 Anne Elder Award and in 2003 the NSW Women Writers National Poetry Prize. In 2004, she was awarded the Martha Richardson Poetry Medal. She runs the Developmental Assessment Program for children and adolescents at the Alfred Hospital, Melbourne. Her new book, *Folly & Grief*, will be published by Melbourne's Black Pepper Press in 2006.

About 'The Taste of Hours' Harrison writes: 'This is a poem of private echoes. Lines and images have been salvaged from previous poems that didn't work or were jettisoned. In its "foldedness" it remains enigmatic to me. I think it is a poem about ennui and depression. How such emotions play with consciousness and how seductive apathy can be.'

MARTIN HARRISON's books of poetry include *Summer* (Paper Bark Press, 2001), *The Kangaroo Farm* (Paper Bark Press, 1997) and *The Distribution of Voice* (UQP, 1993) and a recent sequence of poems, *Music* (Vagabond Press, 2005). A collection of essays, mainly about Australian poetry, was published as *Who Wants to Create Australia?* (Halstead Press, 2004). He teaches writing and poetry at the University of Technology in Sydney.

Harrison writes: 'If I hesitate to say too much about "About the Self", this is because writer's statements all too often get in the way, reducing poetry to the author's intentions. Where these latter are concerned, all I can say is that I am interested in directness, in writing which talks closely and intimately – and in writing which has impact. Of course there are many indirect means to be direct. But that said, closeness, sensoriness, sensation are, to my way of thinking, basic elements in poetry.

'Technically, a lot of my work's explored ways to put more and more information (not the same as more words or things) into the structuring of my poems. So if I don't want my new poems, like "About the Self", to be egotistical or over-riding as can happen with more autobiographical work, I do want them to come clean – I want them to be information-rich and explicit. I suppose any attempt to capture a sensation or a moment in time brings with it the enigma of its context, including the contemporary context – i.e. the moment now in which we are reading the poem. And "About the Self" works in this way no less than some of my poems which are more obviously and clearly focused on natural environments and objects.

'Finally, yes, some of the themes of the poem are obvious: sexual awakening and the formation of intimate forms of seeing and feeling. I would like the poem to be an adequate kind of self-portrait, maybe only one of many and yet momentarily a definitive way of seeing things.'

KEVIN HART's most recent collection is *Flame Tree: Selected Poems* (Bloodaxe/Paper Bark, 2001). After many years teaching at Monash University in Melbourne, he now teaches at the University of Notre Dame in the United States.

Hart writes: 'Some years ago I wrote a poem called "The Word" that is now in my *Flame Tree: Selected Poems*. That poem is about a word that my death will not confide in me but that seems to orient my entire life. I find that my poems explore different, and even contradictory, aspects of experiences, and this poem, "The Word", looks from behind, as it were, at what the earlier poem with the same title explores.'

PHILIP HARVEY is a Melbourne poet and reviewer. He is Poetry Editor of Eureka Street, which changed from inkline to online in May, 2006.

About 'Non-core Promise' Harvey writes: 'Bloomsday in Melbourne is the southern capital's celebration of James Joyce's writing, held annually on the sixteenth of June. I have written many scripts and papers for this literary event over the years, including some using the polylingual masterpiece *Finnegans Wake*. Is Joyce the only person to write in "wakese"? Not at all, in fact Joyce gives freedom to make personal play with his invention. I will never read the book straight through (who has?), but I dip in from all angles, and have read many sequences dozens of times. One effect it has on me is to want to write in "wakese". "Non-Core Promise" is one of a swag of poems written under the influence of this serio-comic novel, but the wordplay is all my own.'

DOMINIQUE HECQ is the author of *The Book of Elsa*, a novel, three collections of stories (*Magic*, *Mythfits* and *Noisy Blood*), two books of poems (*The Gaze of Silence* and *Good Grief*) and two short plays (*One Eye Too Many* and *Cakes & Pains*). *Couch Grass* is forthcoming. Together with Russell Grigg and Craig Smith, she has also co-written *Feminine Sexuality: Freud and the Early Controversies*. She currently teaches in the School of Creative Arts, The University of Melbourne.

Hecq writes: '"Labyrinth" was written to welcome Lydia Ariadne Plastow into the world. This partly explains the mythical references. I was keen to use two voices to celebrate the child's inscription into the world of culture. The darker side, of course, gestures to her inscription in time and history (the reference to the war in Iraq).'

JUDY JOHNSON has published two collections of poetry: *Wing Corrections* and *Nomadic*. A verse novel, *Jack*, will be published by Pandanus Books in September of this year. She teaches creative writing at Newcastle University, and conducts creative-writing workshops.

About 'At the Temple of Sisters' Johnson writes: 'Some

poets feel that certain subject matter shadows them; with me, it's the premature death of members of my family. My poem attempts to capture something of the relationship which can develop between siblings in the face of a terminal illness. The sick sister, in effect, becomes the phantom pulse in the healthy one, the mirror she sees herself reflected in. This twinning is both traumatic and has a monumental intimacy. The temple metaphor is also used to question the notion of self. How ironic that the seemingly solid edifice of ego as we know it, firmly burrowed in the skull, has these two open windows with the thinnest curtains of skin covering them. Why? Is it an invitation to burglars? Or an escape route through which we could perhaps fly out?'

JEAN KENT was born in 1951 in Chinchilla, Queensland, grew up in rural Queensland and now lives at Lake Macquarie, New South Wales. Her three published collections of poetry include *Verandahs,* which won the Anne Elder Prize and the Dame Mary Gilmore Award and was shortlisted for the 1991 New South Wales State Literary Awards, and *The Satin Bowerbird,* which was the winner of the 1998 Wesley Michel Wright Prize. In 1994, she was awarded an Overseas Residency at the Literature Board's Keesing Studio, Paris.

Kent writes: 'Dedicated to my husband, Martin, whose parents migrated to Australia after World War II, "Travelling with the Wrong Phrase Books" is a response to our experiences of going to live in Paris for six months. There was a lot of mind and time travel happening during that short period, but it wasn't until five years later that I was able to start this sequence. After a brief visit to the University of Queensland, where as a student I'd dreamt of living in France, I was at home at Lake Macquarie again, looking at our Paris photos and remembering the struggles to be understood that often accompanied the most basic daily tasks. Other memories swept in, and I began a draft which turned into "First Stop at Photo Station". Originally, the sequence was much longer, incorporating a trip to Lithuania to meet my father-in-law's family. In that form, it won the 2003 Somerset National Poetry Prize. Eventually, though, the Lithuanian part peeled away and developed its own cluster of related poems. So, after considerable revision, the section which was actually the first to be drafted became the end of this poem.'

ANDY KISSANE grew up in Melbourne and moved to Sydney in 1987. He has won the Red Earth Poetry Award, the Harri Jones Memorial Prize and the John Shaw Neilson Poetry Award. He also recently won the inaugural 2005 BTG-*Blue Dog* Poetry Reviewing Competition. He has published two books of poetry, *Facing the Moon* (FIP, 1993) and *Every Night They Dance* (FIP, 2000), and a novel, *Under the Same Sun* (Sceptre, 2000). He teaches creative writing at University of Technology, Sydney, Macquarie University and the University of Western Sydney.

About 'Visiting Melbourne' Kissane writes: 'How many times do we hear our names called out each day? How many times over a lifetime? I don't know, but I have long been fascinated by the incantatory power of names. In my lounge room I listen to Sweet Honey in the Rock call out names as patchwork quilts are laid out on the ground as memorials; I listen as Christy Moore chants the names of the Irish hunger strikers. The names move me just as they did the first time I heard them. There is a power in repetition that we tend to forget as we grow older, and the repeated line is one aspect of the traditional form of the sonnet sequence, the corona, that I love. For my working definition of a corona, I am indebted to Don

Paterson's fine introduction to the anthology he edited, *101 Sonnets from Shakespeare to Heaney* (Faber and Faber, 1999). Thanks to Michelle Lanchester for permission to use her words from "Patchwork Quilt", performed by Sweet Honey in the Rock, Mikkel Music, BMI. Thanks also to Martin Langford, whose poem "Aussie" gave me the idea for the last line of five and the beginning of six. An end can also be a beginning, the corona reminds us, and so it is with family, with old friends, even with death. Writing is another act that must be repeated if it is to prosper, beginning again each day the search for the right words, that struggle to find a way of saying what is most difficult, perhaps even impossible, to say.'

ANTHONY LAWRENCE's most recent book of poems is *The Sleep of a Learning Man* which was shortlisted for *The Age* Book of the Year Award, for the Victorian Premier's Award, and the Tasmania Prize.

Lawrence writes: '"Equation" was written after reading a journal on mathematics, where bubble-trees and ghost-prints mutate into poetry. I still loathe working with all things numerical, but the language used to define whatever it is they're talking about threw me headfirst into the poem. The birds and insects kept things in order, as did meditation.'

EMMA LEW has published two volumes of poetry: *The Wild Reply* (Black Pepper, 1997), and *Anything the Landlord Touches* (Giramondo, 2002). She lives in Melbourne.

About 'Finishing School' Lew writes: 'I don't know what I started out trying to do in this poem. It ended up a dark little "olde world" monologue, the portrait of a woman both obsessed and calm.'

KATE LLEWELLYN has published seventeen books. She is the co-editor of *The Penguin Book of Australian Women's Poetry* and has published seven books of poetry. She has written four travel books on India and Italy, on New Zealand and the Cook Islands, and on East Africa and Australia. Her book *The Waterlily's Blue Mountain Journal* was a best seller and has sold over 30,000 copies in Australia and was made into a talking book. *Playing With Water* (which is nature writing and memoir) is her most recent book, published by HarperCollins in 2005. She is the recipient of a Senior Writer's Fellowship from the Literature Board and is currently writing her autobiography.

About 'Tongue' Llewellyn writes: 'I wrote the poem on a holiday on an orchard in Queensland. I was thinking about the power and danger of language and how glorious it is. I thought of those great writers mentioned in the poem and, being on a farm, I suppose I was feeling bucolic and thought of horses. There was a lake and a river on the farm, the Tallebudgera River, and poems seem to me to come from a river or a lake in the mind. Perhaps it rose from that lake called Dahlia Pearl which is not on any map. Who can say? It rolled off my tongue like a pebble.'

KATHRYN LOMER has a background in teaching ESL. Her book of poetry, *Extraction of Arrows*, won the 2003 Anne Elder Award for a first collection. Her other books are a novel, *The God in the Ink*, and a novel for young adults, *The Spare Room*. All are published by UQP.

About 'Sorrow of the Women' Lomer writes: 'A broadcast of Radio National's *Lingua Franca* prompted this poem. The program was about the script called Nushu, used by women in Hunan province in China until it was outlawed by the state in the 1950s. With a background in linguistics, I was fascinated by the concept of a gender-specific script.'

KATE MIDDLETON is a Melbourne writer. Her poems have previously appeared in many journals and newspapers including *ABR*, *Heat*, *Meanjin*, *Tinfish* (US), *The Age* and *The Australian*.

About 'Aftermath' Middleton writes: 'This poem is the third "voice" of *The Juniper Quartet*, written around the Grimm fairytale *The Juniper Tree*. Each poem in the quartet represents the voice of each main character: father, stepmother, son and daughter. This poem is the father's approach to the story. The quartet was written as a birthday present for my dear friend Dr Molly Williams.

'*The Juniper Tree* is one of the most bloody of the fairytales collected by the brothers Grimm. In the story a stepmother kills her stepson, and then allows her natural daughter to believe she is responsible for her half-brother's death. Echoing classical mythology, the stepmother cooks the boy and his father eats him. In the second half the boy returns in the persona of a bird to exact revenge. After his stepmother's death he is resurrected, and his family is reformed.'

PETER MINTER is a poet, editor and reviewer living in Sydney, where he teaches Indigenous Studies at the Koori Centre, University of Sydney. His *Empty Texas* won the 2000 *Age* Poetry Book of the Year, and he was poetry editor of *Meanjin* from 2000–2005. His new book *blue grass* is published by Salt Publishing. Please visit peterminter.org.

Minter writes: 'Serine is "a colourless, crystalline amino-acid which is widely distributed in animal proteins" (OED). The poem was conceived after a cold, clear, very windy but serene winter's night, as I lay in bed and watched moonlight rush through the branches and long seed pods of a tree by my window. The spirit of the night was alive in the tree, and I remembered the many times, often outside at night in the bush, when I'd seen distant hills and forests awash under the full moon and wind, bright clouds racing by. In the morning I found seed pods and seeds scattered over the grass and path, and I reflected on the beautiful mechanics of life, the deathly cold wind causing the pods to fall, some opening themselves to scatter their seeds to the earth, some staying closed forever. On holding the closed seed pods to the light I could see the little black seeds lined up through the skin, like a karyotype of lines of chromosomes – thus the poem's title. At the time I was closely reading the poems of Jorie Graham, and "Serine" speaks to her beautiful study of similar organic patterns, "The Geese".'

DAVID MUSGRAVE has published three books of poetry: *To Thalia* (2004), *On Reflection* (2005) and *Watermark* (2006). He has two collections forthcoming: *Bodies of Water*, in collaboration with his partner, the photographer Fe Robards, and the other collecting his poems from the past four years.

About 'Young Montaigne Goes Riding' Musgrave writes: 'I first wrote a version of this poem in 1990 after an extensive infatuation with Montaigne's essays, but found it deficient in terms of its rhymes and the persona itself, and shelved it for a while. I picked it up again in 2002 and began to re-work it after reading a new, bilingual edition of Montaigne's essays. Direct access to the French enabled me to have a clearer idea of the persona I was trying to develop. The concept of the essay, as a literary form, as an aesthetic and as an ethical position seemed to be perfectly suited to a semi-aimless horse ride, in rhyme, with the elegant persona of a younger Montaigne easing into that of the essayist. Redeveloping the poem along these lines was what really enabled me to complete it satisfactorily. Nearly all of the imagery comes directly from Montaigne's essays.'

JASON NELSON is a lecturer of Digital Writing and Art at Griffith University. His digital/cyber poems have appeared in galleries and journals across the world. But he still plays in print occasionally.

About 'How the Sun Works' Nelson writes: 'The sun scares me. Something about the solar explosions, they seem aware of their patterns, their heat and spindled reach. During one of those eclipse-watching parties where people use cardboard blinders to watch the sun darken away, I noticed tiny shadows churning at the sphere's edge. They appeared to be working, what seemed to be arms connected to pipes and wires. The poem was built from this brief sighting of the sun's secret comptrollers. Initially this wasn't written in line break form and instead occupied a prose poem block. But enjambment always makes words multidirectional, hypertextual in a way, and so some clumsy chopping led the poem to this awkward stable. Oddly enough, this poem also exists as a cyberpoem, complete with moving bits and grinder sounds. And although my current career (secrettechnology.com) is mostly as a digital poet, with much more in animated and interactive states than cellulose, I do find these words blend better on the bendable page.'

JOHN NIJJEM is a writer who has published work in poetry as well as articles on a wide number of philosophical and theoretical issues. He lives and works in Sydney and is currently co-editing a book about the future of literature and literary criticism, while completing a PhD in philosophy in the area of the phenomenology of selfhood.

Nijjem writes: '"At Turin" began as part of a suite of poems tentatively entitled "Horses". The suite deals with a number of broadly theological themes but always with the archetypal – tutelary, "paschal" or numinous – presence of horses (a presence literal, metonymic, anagogic) somewhere in the peripheries. In "At Turin", the image of the horse, at once mundane and mythic, gathers senses that specifically show up under the aspect of Nietzsche's intense religious and ontological concerns – concerns which, for me, largely centre on something to do with the enigma of a passivity and incorrigibility at the base of all suffering. The poem attends to this legendary almost hagiographical episode in Nietzsche's narrative as if the event were itself a kind of symbol. Ultimately the image of the horse seems to operate in these poems as a marker for that which is between representation and reality or between the judgment of others and the judgment of self and, indeed, as in Nietzsche's case, between sanity and insanity and thus as a daimonic figure both liminal and eschatological.'

JAN OWEN is a South Australian poet who lives next to coastal scrubland south of Adelaide. Her fifth book, *Timedancing*, was published by Five Islands Press in 2002. She takes up any chance to travel and many of her recent poems come from the experience of finding herself wonderfully lost.

About 'Through Kersenmarkt' Owen writes: 'I was in the Netherlands in 2002 for the Maastricht Poetry Nights and I remember this young woman as the still centre of the city; my memories of the place radiate out from her presence on that bridge. It was strangely reassuring to see her sitting there each day, somehow sweetening irony. The meaning of her music became part of the music of meaning. As I drafted and redrafted the poem the closed "m", "n", and "ng" sounds weighed in against the sibilants, and half rhymes arrived irregularly, so perhaps the muted resonance and the lightly connected lines echo the subject.'

DOROTHY PORTER's most recent publication is the chap-book *Poems: January to August 2004* from Vagabond Press. In 2005 she wrote the lyrics for *Before Time Could Change Us* – a music CD collaboration with Paul Grabowsky and Katie Noonan, from Warner Records, which won the ARIA for Best Jazz Album.

Porter writes: '"Waterview Street" is one of my rare directly autobiographical poems. It is about both a real and haunted place – Waterview Street in Mona Vale where I grew up and my parents still live. When I visit my parents I have a favour-ite walk down to Winji Jimi Park on Pittwater, where a very dear friend of my mother's and mine used to live. This poem is about the absolute mystery at the heart of being alive – and not being alive. And how being alive is about other lives, how you walk through them, as well as your own.'

PETER PORTER edited last year's *Best Australian Poetry* and continues to publish poems in Australia and the UK, where he lives. Born in Brisbane in 1929, he is the author of more than twenty books of poems and is a freelance writer and broad-caster. His most recent collection was *Afterburner* (Picador, 2004).

About 'The Last Gruppetti' Porter writes: 'I like to write music criticism in the form of poetry. Gruppetti are turns of phrase in the manner of *appoggiature*, tightly ordered groups of notes which swing a melody on to another course. Wagner used them in his compositions throughout his career: they are highly characteristic of his style, as they were also of his pred-ecessor and model Weber. In my second stanza I recall an old ice-cream vendor who sold cones of ice-cream from a horse and cart just outside our school gates when I was a boarder in Toowoomba. He must have been born not very far from the Austro-Hungarian domains. Montsalvat is the legendary home of the Order of Knights in Wagner's *Parsifal*, an opera pervaded by the idea of redemption, although Wagner was never an orthodox Christian. Wagner's obsessive chromaticism, especially in *Tristan und Isolde* and *Parsifal*, changed the course of European music. The poem considers the turns of Wagnerian melody as being on the path of the descent of the dove of Grace. But our day-to-day life (second stanza) marks the point at which life and death are located, and which art and redemption must serve. An odd poem, I would concede.'

PETER ROSE is currently the editor of *Australian Book Review*. His most recent collection is *Rattus Rattus: New and Selected Poems* (Salt, 2005). Other publications include *Rose Boys* (Allen & Unwin, 2001), which won the 2003 National Biography Award, and a novel, *A Case of Knives* (Allen & Unwin, 2005).

About 'Beach Burial' Rose writes: 'My friend Craig Sherborne and I lost our fathers (curious, apt phrase) within a year of each other, and both of us, almost of necessity, have written a number of elegies. "Beach Burial" was prompted by Craig's verbal account of the remarkable, Byronic circumstances in which he dispersed his father's ashes in the sea. Craig went on to write a memorable poem on the subject, but I don't feel too contrite about my trespass, for death and loss are capable of infinite shadings and meanings. In the end, my poem comes back to the tidal shifts of mourning and to one's own feelings of lostness, emptiness and silencing.'

GIG RYAN is the author of *The Division of Anger* (1981), *Manners of an Astronaut* (1984), *The Last Interior* (1986), *Excavation* (1990), *Pure and Applied* (1998) and *Heroic Money* (2001). She is currently working on a selected poems, and a new book of poems. She has written songs with occasional band Driving Past on *Real Estate* (Chapter Music, 1999) and *Travel* (Jacana, 2006). She is poetry editor at *The Age* and a freelance reviewer.

About 'Kangaroo and Emu' Ryan writes: 'This poem began during the 2004 Federal election campaign, and was completed in its aftermath. "The tree of…" is the Tree of Knowledge in Barcaldine, Queensland, which refers to the founding of the Australian Labor Party.'

PHILIP SALOM's most recent collections are *The Well Mouth*, which follows a novel, *Toccata and Rain* (shortlisted for the ALS Gold Medal), and *A Cretive Life*. Recent recognition of his work includes the Christopher Brennan Award and an Australia Council Writers Fellowship.

About 'The Man with a Shattered World' Salom writes: 'The story of Zasetsky's extraordinary passion to use writing as a means to recover a "self" so (irrevocably) undermined by amnesias, attracted me from the first pages of A R Luria's book. Most people seek an expansion or intensification of perception, and therefore fear *reduction*, but we know it stalks us, through illness, trauma or even just old age – thus the unsettling nature of this young man's ruin. But Zasetsky surely is unique: except for the shortest words, each word he wrote was longer than his field of vision. He was forced to scan backwards to re-read what he had only just written. A terrible travel/travail of identity, and struggle. Then, a day later, all forgotten, he would start again. Truly a Sisyphean existence and one highlighting extremes of courage and pathos. I bracket irrevocably (above) out of the irony of his case: he desperately hoped he would improve but his brain injuries were permanent.'

ALEX SKOVRON is the author of four collections of poetry: *The Rearrangement* (1988), *Sleeve Notes* (1992), *Infinite City* (1999), and *The Man and the Map* (2003). His most recent book is a prose novella, *The Poet* (2005). He lives in Melbourne and works as a freelance book editor. 'Sorcery' is part of a book-length manuscript of prose-poems awarded the 2005 Wesley Michel Wright Prize for Poetry.

Of 'Sorcery', Skovron writes: 'In the second half of 2002, and then again throughout 2004, my writing was focused almost entirely on prose-poetry. Each of the 140-odd pieces I wrote over that period is in the form of a single justified paragraph block of around 250 words. Embracing a variety of subjects and voices, the poems explore memory, language, eros and the affections, the nature of narrative, and our shifting perspectives on "reality". I am very interested in the musical and rhythmic possibilities of prose; in this case, I included rhyme to intensify the poem's rhetorical, incantatory drive.'

KATHLEEN STEWART was born in Sydney in 1958. She has published two collections of poetry: *Snow* and *The White Star*. She has also published seven novels: *Waiting Room*, *Victim Train*, *Louis: A Normal Novel*, *Spilt Milk*, *Nightflowers*, *The Red Room*, and *The Black Butterfly*.

About 'How I Got Away' Stewart writes: 'I wrote this poem looking back on the difficult end of a relationship and its aftermath. I use here a personal mythology of sorts, that draws imagery from the Rider-Waite tarot deck and reverses fragments of the myth of Persephone.'

MARIA TAKOLANDER is a lecturer in Literary Studies at Deakin University in Geelong and the author of a chapbook of poems, *Narcissism* (Whitmore Press, 2005). 'Storm' was shortlisted for the inaugural 2005 *Australian Book Review* Poetry Prize.

Takolander writes: '"Storm" was inspired by a landscape painting by Terry Eichler, which portrays the sublime vision of a storm taking over the sky and the earth as if something from the gods. It made me think about how small we are, about how mysterious the world is, and about all of the things we forget. The uncanny, according to Freud, is the anxious experience of sensing those things we have forgotten, those things we cannot know, those things we do not want to know. However, it's an erotic experience, too. The uncanny describes not only a terrible recognition of something but also a carnal awakening to something. The anxiety and eroticism, the terror and the beauty, conjured by the forgotten or the repressed is something I'm interested in. I like the uncanny.'

BARBARA TEMPERTON (aka Barbara Brandt) was born and raised in Western Australia. Her first collection of poems, *The Snow Queen Takes Lunch in the Station Café*, appeared in *Shorelines* (FACP, 1995). In 2000, she participated in the Poetry Mentor Programme – an eight-day intensive live-in mentorship programme with Dorothy Porter at the Varuna Writers Centre, Katoomba, New South Wales. Temperton's second collection, *Going Feral* (FACP, 2002), won the 2002 West Australian Premier's Book Award for Poetry. 'The Lighthouse Keeper's Wife' won the 2002 Tom Collins Poetry Prize. She is currently completing an MA in Creative Writing with the University of Western Australia.

About 'The Lighthouse Keeper's Wife' Temperton writes: 'I'm in the fifth and final year of my degree. Over that period I've written very few short works, wrestling instead with the long narrative poems that comprise the creative component.

"The Lighthouse Keeper's Wife" is a kind of maquette: a smaller version of one of those large poems. Coming from the north, I've lived in Albany at the edge of the Southern Ocean for nearly ten years. The Point King Lighthouse is one of my favourite places here. Built in 1857 – just above the channel between Princess Royal Harbour and the gorgeous, often unpredictable, King George Sound – the lighthouse is now a ruin. The characters and events of "The Lighthouse Keeper's Wife" are imaginary, but they arose from my fascination with what remains of the old cottage that once housed the light tower; its location; the keepers, their wives and children, and the folklore surrounding them all.'

CHRIS WALLACE-CRABBE is a poet, essayist and former director of The Australian Centre at Melbourne University. He has published thirteen collections of verse, as well as a number of artists' books. His *Selected Poems 1956–1994* (OUP, 1995) won the *Age* Book of the Year Prize and the D J O'Hearn Prize for Poetry. His most recent books are *The Universe Looks Down* (Brandl & Schlesinger, 2005) and a critical volume, *Read It Again* (Salt, 2005).

About 'The Alignments' Wallace-Crabbe writes: 'For a dozen years I have been producing those beautiful, expensive objects known as artists' books with the Melbourne artist Bruno Leti. Much of his work has linear configuration, so at one point I undertook a suite based on the roles that are played by lines in our thinking and perception. Later, while on a residency at Bundanon, I met the Sydney composer Damien Ricketson and we began to work towards a collaboration: this became the experimental work for various instruments and voices, "A Line Has Two", which was performed at the Studio, Sydney Opera House, to my astonishment and pleasure. Of course, I had long been fascinated by my daughter's infant question, "Why do things have a line round them?".'

LESLEY WALTER is a Sydney poet whose collection *watermelon baby* was published by Five Islands Press in 2000. Her awards include the Dame Leonie Kramer Prize in Australian Poetry from the University of Sydney in 1996, The Society of Women Writers New South Wales Poetry Prize in 2000 and the Gwen Harwood Poetry Prize in 2004.

About 'Hyphenated Lives' Walter writes: 'I had read an article about the cojoined Bunker twins in a newspaper some years ago, and, fascinated, had cut it out and filed it away. As subjects for poems tend to do, however, this one possessed some small recess in my mind from that time on until finally, years later, I had to sit down and write it out. What intrigued me then – and intrigues me still – was/is the fact of these twins having been able to engage, joined as they were, in intimate, sexual relationships; and their having fathered so many children between them. The imagined nature of those relationships seemed to defy all my own acculturated notions of intimacy, marriage and parenthood. Yet in writing about them, they appeared almost, if not entirely "normal", which of course, in the circumstances, they were. The notion, too, of one of the twins having had to confront his own imminent death upon the demise of his brother, had struck me as particularly poignant; as did the twins' seemingly buoyant, brave and well-adjusted natures in the face of what to many would be a limiting, if not wholly incapacitating, condition. I hope the poem has managed to bring some small part of its subjects back to life.'

MEREDITH WATTISON was born in 1963. Her four books of poetry are *Psyche's Circus* (Poetry Australia, 1989), *Judith's*

Do, as part of a three-poet volume, *Conversations of Love* (Penguin, 1996), *Fishwife* (FIP, 2001) and *The Nihilist Line* (FIP, 2003). Her new work, which contains 'Ibsen's Fawn,' is in the pipeline and titled *Basket of Sunlight*.

About 'Ibsen's Fawn' Wattison writes: 'This poem was written from 8-11 August, 2004. It began with "He is an Ibsenism" and the rest flowed. The poem itself was written quite quickly; on my first drafts there is little change, the most work was done on its title. Its first title was "Gripping Beast"; among a list of another eighteen are "Throat Singing", "The Tongue's Seat", "His Edible Mistress". The final title came about by being playful with the use of the word "fawn". It was a social act, not an animal, and by ear, also some kind of incredible, rampant creature possessing both sincerity and guile.

'In this poem the ruse is obvious, known and celebrated. The dog's skills are admired. References to human history and social standing are there for narrative credibility and the sheer, mouth, ear enjoyment of them.'

SIMON WEST was born in 1974 in Melbourne where he currently teaches in Italian Studies. In 2004 he held a Poets Union Australian Young Poets Fellowship. His first collection of poetry will be published in September 2006 with Puncher & Wattmann (puncherandwattmann.com).

About '*I giorni della merla*' West writes: 'I wrote this poem a few years ago when I lived in Turin. *I giorni della merla* are the last three days of January. Traditionally they mark the coldest point of the Italian winter, after which the blackbird knows that it is time to start making her nest.'

Series Editors' Biographies

Bronwyn Lea was born in Tasmania, grew up in Queensland and Papua New Guinea, and lived in California for twelve years. She is the author of *Flight Animals* (UQP, 2001), which won the Wesley Michel Wright Prize for Poetry, the Fellowship of Australian Writers Anne Elder Award, and was shortlisted for a number of other prizes. She is currently the Poetry Editor at University of Queensland Press and lectures in Poetics and Narrative at the University of Queensland.

Martin Duwell was born in England and has lived in Australia since 1957. He was a publisher and critic of contemporary Australian poetry in the seventies and eighties and since that time has written widely on the subject in essays and reviews. As poetry reviewer for *The Australian* from 1989–1998 he reviewed over 130 books of verse. He is the author of a set of interviews with poets, *A Possible Contemporary Poetry* (Makar, 1982) and, with R M W Dixon, is the editor of two anthologies of Aboriginal song poetry: *The Honey-Ant Men's Love* Song (UQP, 1990) and *Little Eva at Moonlight Creek* (UQP, 1994). He has also edited an edition of the *Selected Poems of John Blight* and was one of the editors of the *Penguin New Literary History of Australia* (Penguin, 1988). He has a strong interest in medieval Icelandic literature and Persian language and literature.

Journals Where the Poems First Appeared

The Age, poetry ed. Gig Ryan. 250 Spencer Street, Melbourne, VIC 3000.

The Australian Book Review, ed. Peter Rose. PO Box 2320, Richmond South, VIC 3121.

Blast Magazine, ed. Ann Nugent. PO Box 134, Campbell, ACT 2612.

Blue Dog: Australian Poetry, ed. Ron Pretty. c/o Poetry Australia. PO Box U34, Wollongong University, NSW 2500.

Famous Reporter, ed. Ralph Wessman. PO Box 368, North Hobart, TAS 7002.

Griffith Review, literary ed. Nigel Krauth. Griffith University, University Drive, Meadowbrook, QLD 4131.

Heat, poetry ed. Lucy Dougan. Dean's Unit, CAESS, University of Western, Sydney, Locked Bag 1797, Penrith South DC, NSW 1797.

Island, ed. Peter Owen. PO Box 210, Sandy Bay, TAS 7006.

Meanjin, poetry ed. Judith Beveridge. 131 Barry Street, Carlton, VIC 3053.

Southerly, ed. David Brooks. Department of English, Woolley Building A20, University of Sydney, NSW 2006.

Space: New Writing, ed. Anthony Lynch. PO Box 833, Geelong, VIC 3220.

The Weekend Australian, ed. Barry Hill. GPO Box 4245, Sydney, NSW 2001.

Westerly, ed. Delys Bird and Dennis Haskell. English, Communication and Cultural Studies, The University of Western Australia, Crawley, WA 6009.

Acknowledgments

The general editors would like to thank Carol Hetherington and Natalie Seger for their research assistance with this book. Grateful acknowledgment is made to the following publications from which the poems in this volume were chosen:

Robert Adamson, 'A Visitation.' *The Weekend Australian* 31 Dec 2005–1 Jan 2006 Review: 13.

Luke Beesley, 'The Fight.' *Heat* 10 NS (2005): 232–33.

Judith Bishop, 'Rabbit.' *Australian Book Review* 270 (Apr, 2005): 19.

Stephen Edgar, 'Man on the Moon.' *Australian Book Review* 270 (Apr, 2005): 13.

Danny Gentile, 'The Lenten Veil.' *Meanjin* 64.1–2 (2005): 113.

Jane Gibian, 'Ardent.' *Heat* 9 NS (2005): 187.

Kevin Gillam, 'Low at the Edge of the Sands.' *Australian Book Review* 269 (Mar, 2005): 26.

Alan Gould, 'Iris.' *Blue Dog: Australian Poetry* 4.7 (2005): 23.

Philip Hammial, 'Water.' *Famous Reporter* 31 (2005): 97.

Jennifer Harrison, 'The Taste of Hours.' *Blast Magazine* 2 NS (2005): 23.

Martin Harrison, 'About the Self.' *Meanjin* 64.1–2 (2005): 158–59.

Kevin Hart, 'The Word.' *Space: New Writing* 2 (2005): 48.

Philip Harvey, 'Non-core Promise.' *Blue Dog: Australian Poetry* 4.8 (2005): 42.

Dominique Hecq, 'Labyrinth.' *Island* 101 (2005): 84–85.

Judy Johnson, 'At the Temple of Sisters.' *Blue Dog: Australian Poetry* 4.7 (2005): 55–56.

Jean Kent, 'Travelling with the Wrong Phrase Books.' *Westerly* 50 (2005): 146–150.

Andy Kissane, 'Visiting Melbourne.' *Griffith Review* (Summer 2005–2006): 161–62.

Anthony Lawrence, 'Equation.' *Australian Book Review* 274 (Sept, 2005): 35.

Emma Lew, 'Finishing School.' *Heat* 9 NS (2005): 228.

Kate Llewellyn, 'Tongue.' *Southerly* 65.1 (2005): 34.

Kathryn Lomer, 'Sorrow of the Women.' *Space: New Writing* 2 (2005): 9–10.

Kate Middleton, 'Aftermath (Grief).' *The Weekend Australian* 27–28 Aug 2005 Review: 10.

Peter Minter, 'Serine.' *Island* 102 (2005): 96–97.

David Musgrave, 'Young Montaigne Goes Riding.' *Blue Dog: Australian Poetry* 4.7 (2005): 19–22.

Jason Nelson, 'How the Sun Works.' *Meanjin*, 64.1–2 (2005): 311.

John Nijjem, 'At Turin.' *Meanjin* 64.3 (2005): 14.

Jan Owen, 'Through Kersenmarkt.' *Blast Magazine* 2 NS (2005): 7.

Dorothy Porter, 'Waterview Street.' *Australian Book Review* 276 (Nov, 2005): 34.

Peter Porter, 'The Last Gruppetti.' *Australian Book Review* 271 (May, 2005): 49.

Peter Rose, 'Beach Burial.' *Australian Book Review* 275 (Oct, 2005): 31.

Gig Ryan, 'Kangaroo and Emu.' *Heat* 9 NS (2005): 123–24.

Philip Salom, from 'The Man with a Shattered World.' *Westerly* 50 (2005): 201–04.

Alex Skovron, 'Sorcery.' *Meanjin* 64.3 (2005): 5.

Kathleen Stewart, 'How I Got Away.' *Meanjin* 64.1 (2005): 324–25.

Maria Takolander, 'Storm.' *Australian Book Review* 269 (Mar, 2005): 23.

Barbara Temperton, 'The Lighthouse Keeper's Wife.' *Westerly* 50 (2005): 199–200.

Chris Wallace-Crabbe, 'The Alignments.' *Heat* 9 NS (2005): 252–55.

Lesley Walter, 'Hyphenated Lives.' *Island* 101 (2005): 96–99.

Meredith Wattison, 'Ibsen's Fawn.' *Meanjin* 64.3 (2005): 20.

Simon West, '*I giorni della merla.*' *Famous Reporter* 31 (2005): 58.

THE JOSEPHINE ULRICK POETRY PRIZE 2007

The Josephine Ulrick and Win Schubert Foundation for the Arts
are the proud sponsors of Australia's richest poetry prize.
It is named in memory of Josephine Ulrick
whose three great loves were art, literature and photography.

FIRST PRIZE – $10,000
AWARDED TO A POEM OR SUITE OF POEMS UP TO TWO HUNDRED LINES

For prize dates and conditions of entry contact:
The Josephine Ulrick Poetry Prize 2007
Attention Virginia D Boskovic
School Secretary, Arts
Gold Coast Campus Griffith University
PMB 50, Gold Coast Mail Centre, Qld 9726, Australia
Phone: 07 5552 8410
E-mail: v.boskovic@griffith.edu.au

PREVIOUS WINNERS OF THE JOSEPHINE ULRICK POETRY PRIZE
2006: Nathan Shepherdson
2005: Chris Fontana
2004: Nathan Shepherdson
2003: Judith Beveridge
2002: Judy Johnson
2001: Anthony Lawrence
2000: Kathryn Lomer
1999: Jean Kent

The winning entry for 2006 follows.

Nathan Shepherdson

TO FIND WHAT IS NOT THERE

you have reached the end of this poem
and this poem will come to an end when you have ended

to measure the distance from yourself to yourself
you must think of what can be removed without measurement

if you continue to read these words
you will bone the carcass of its thoughts

so there is opportunity to remove the thought from the content
to have the hand dislodge the fibres from sleeping teeth

thoughts swing easily from retinal lips
fertilising each absence as it falls into your own beautiful
        stone hand

you can decide what will happen
by simply describing what you will see

then your eyes will be placed in a petri dish
and you will wait for them to grow into each other

so if you can see to the end of this sentence
you are either lying or you are blind

even the most basic words in repetition
make their own time one time in all time

just now you are writing your own bible in your own saliva
but you must drink the words while they are warm

self fund the research into every species of doubt
this from the vantage point of a white ant inside the heart

the insect is the munificent king to its purpose
it folds its short life into the longest evolution

and if there is one theory then there is one theory too many
and you must believe what you say only until you say it

there is someone else and it is yourself
you discern the pulse by putting your ear to the door

and yet you worship with fascination what you cannot hear
in this instance the fly's six legs landing on your arm

it is the last day of the year
and thousands of ears will wash up onto the beach

you are one of the few with a licence to collect them
because you have the skills to produce a bruise with a whisper

each morning you descend the five steps

apply revisionist principles to clouds rolling across your
    tongue

your feet make uncertain movements on this floor made of
    skin
managing to step outside the accepted path but inside this line

there is an economy based solely on the price of the full stop
there is a full stop with its price fixed on the value of your life

being perfectly still
you remind yourself of the only reason that this reason could be

nothing exists because you exist
you exist because nothing exists as a word in this sentence

still perfectly still
as still as the word that put a spell on itself then died

so make sure the word is dead
before you kneel down to pick it up

and make sure that the word feels balanced in your hand
before you cast it as the first stone

language is original sin
and you are this sentence written in that language

there is inside this idea
only the one idea which you will be unable to realise

words are burned and dumped at the corners of your lips
the ashes mixed disparagingly with letters from this unreadied
     quote

the air confesses its intent to you to make you breathe
to inflate your limbs with its alluvial ether

you are no longer honest because you tell the truth
there is in this message everything that is known

hesitation stands over your body at night
recording the frequency and duration of the glow on your
     eyelids

you have multiple heads which are dispersed through your
     sleep
they end up on a tray as finger food for the clock

you sleep in a finite kingdom fumigated with cold charity
you wake to the blessing of company unknown

under the bedclothes of a single comma
lives the soul ←

you ask the moment to put its clothes back on

take a few steps back then realise your lungs are full of
     sunlight

this is an untitled complexity unbuttoning its collar
revealing to you the two clean holes at the base of the neck

it is unlikely that what will happen next will happen at all
the surest path to anything is the one you have just left

the future will not visit you today
due to unavoidable circumstance it needs to spend time alone

you are in possession of a straight line with a switch at either
     end
but the straight line cannot be drawn on its faults

you are the possession of a straight line with a switch at either
     end
the line you discovered straight after your mother's death

as a child your mother used to plait your eyelashes
crimp the ritual by singeing each one with a match

you taught yourself to foreshorten fragments in domestic
     space
to smooth these sheets of light growing into an organic lens

you became famous for your paintings of blank walls

these the incessant attempts to erase this self portrait

should the painting tell a story or tell how it was painted
this painting that paints the painter with its hands over the
      painter's eyes

you have been requested to land on these marks made by this
      blunt pencil
to slow down your progress by yielding to acceleration

despite what was advertised this is not about consensus
it's about trying to match your fingerprints against stains on a
      foreign wall

the precondition is that you mould each face into a candle
set each one alight then put each one out with your tongue

yesterday you put a hammer and some nails into the boot of
      your car
today you empty your pockets of loose change to pay for your
      resurrection

you kill the purpose to save the device that served the purpose
inside this container of distraction is uncontained distraction

adequate signage is provided for your inadequacies
sarcastic thunder bowling unexploded laughter at your feet

this is a hospital for unsatisfied dreams
where personality is fitted with prosthetics for the new
    century

this is a quaint comedy where your ego is towed out to sea
and scuttled unceremoniously for use as an artificial reef

it is well known that fingers will float in a bowl of tears
that the lighthouse in the conscience actually attracts pain

off the loom you study the warp and weft of these fingers
    enmeshed
this cloth that is cut into uncreased garments of pure sensation

you are compelled to lick the blood off simple anxieties
in order to feel at peace

you are compelled to put your blood in a kettle
and count how many bodies appear in the steam

memories can only be repaired with the blood from an unused lie
and you have just used the last unused lie known to exist

memory is an uncollating centrifuge
pinning stretched images onto its inner wall

and the objects on this escalator called recognition
are only humid prototypes abandoned in the designer's mind

you stare at a large orange on a black plate
soft citrus granite impersonating an ovum from the sun

you listen to the perfect elastic syllable of a chorus of bees
as they attack efflorescence and its face solid with new
      imagination

on the precipice you become the rain falling into your open
      mouth
you wash yourself into crevices pool yourself on the basalt
      crust

your ghosts will sing if they are asked to
but you must draw a picture of a mouth for their mouths to
      sing to

to sing to your mouth requires that you know which mouth is
      yours
and on your say so every song known has just ended

although you know how to stencil words onto moths' wings
and you know it is only possible to let them go in the dark

a bottle of lactic acid is being consumed in quiet celebration
because you are running to the end of this circular sentence

there is no evidence in this sentence
because you solved the crime when you committed the crime

to deny space you must accept your absence
inseminate yourself with unrepeatable echoes doused in wine

you take meaning to a point where you are taken by the
    meaning
and this is too far and not far enough

you take turns and in turn are taken nowhere
to where your shadow licks the salt from your chest

shadows beg you for light as you walk down the street
and you oblige by spitting reflection into their misshapen tin
    cups

the shadow from each day is preserved in an unlit freezer
and is taken out as a prayer mat each night

one voice will call and one voice will say nothing
and you will hear both voices at once

the art is to destroy clarity with more clarity
to put one word in a room and watch it fight with itself

to find what is not there
you must look for what is not there